Laura,

Thank

Guest Bed

Luke P. Narlee

Luke P. Narlee/Take Exit 3 Publishing
www.narleebooks.com
www.narleebooks@gmail.com

Printed and Bound in the United States of America

Book Layout © 2016 BookDesignTemplates.com

Cover Design © 2016 by Vanessa Mendozzi

Guest Bed/ Luke P. Narlee.—1st edition
ISBN-13: 978-0-692-78699-4
ISBN-10: 0-692-78699-6

I'd like to thank Peter T. McQueeny for convincing me that this story was "too good" to leave as a short/side story within a different book.

For all the married couples; past, present, and future.

CONTENTS

THE SILVER KEY DINER, 1989 1

MORNING REFLECTION 3

BREAKFAST 9

THE BOOKSTORE, 1989 33

THE ACCIDENT 39

STRANGER DANGER? 49

THE ARRANGEMENT 79

HOME SWEET HOME 101

EVENING DISCUSSION 115

THE GUEST BED 129

FRESH START 141

BACK AT THE OFFICE 157

THE SATELLITE RESTAURANT, 1989 171

DEJA VU 175

HAPPY ANNIVERSARY 183

THE RETURN 203

THE OTHER WOMAN 211

THE MORNING AFTER 221

SURPRISE VISIT 235

FINAL EVENING ALONE 253

Guest Bed

Part 1

"After a few years of marriage, a man can look right at a woman without seeing her—and a woman can see right through a man without looking at him."

— HELEN ROWLAND

"How can a woman be expected to be happy with a man who insists on treating her as if she were a perfectly normal human being."

— OSCAR WILDE

CHAPTER ONE

THE SILVER KEY DINER, 1989

For our first date, I took Kate downtown to the Silver Key Diner where she spent ninety minutes holding me captive with her sparkling brown eyes. She wore a loose-fitting white sundress patterned with bright yellow sunflowers. The way her shimmering hair fell forward over her bare shoulders made my heart race.

Neither one of us was hungry, so we settled for coffee. Our new attraction had replaced the need for sustenance.

"Katherine Hoffman," I said, reaching across the table and taking her hand in mine, "you are, without a doubt, the most adorable thing I've ever laid eyes on."

Her cheeks flushed, a wild pink rose. "Kate," she replied. "It's just Kate. But, thank you."

I leaned back and studied her with caution as she fidgeted with her lip gloss, pulling the cap on and off. I became anxious—worried that I had confessed too much. Was she disappointed that I had said her name wrong?

A couple of minutes later, the waiter dropped off the check. I fumbled as I signed my name on the receipt, unsure of where things were headed. Then, as we stood to leave, Kate leaned over the table—practically tipping over our empty cups—and kissed me.

CHAPTER TWO

MORNING REFLECTION

Lying on my side, I reach behind me and feel across the mattress to verify what I already know to be true: I'm alone. I roll onto my back and examine the empty space beside me. A complex design comprised of wrinkled sheets and dented pillows lingers in Kate's absence.

I shift my eyes toward the bathroom. Door half open, full of shadows, still brimming with remnants of last night's darkness.

Our twelfth wedding anniversary is less than twenty-four hours away, and for the first time since we were married, I have nothing planned. No diamonds, no flowers, no reservations. Every time I try to conjure up a decent idea, my mind goes blank. Do gifts and romantic dinners still mean something when we barely speak to one another? When we're just going through the motions, watching yet another day pass by and disappear with all the others that failed to add shape or color to our lives?

Last night, Kate's mother came by and picked up the girls. Leaving us with the house to ourselves for a few days was her anniversary gift to us, and we accepted it gratefully. We had hoped that the lack of distractions would do us good. Give us time to talk and hash things out. But, unsurprisingly, things didn't go as planned. Not that anything bad happened; it was more that, as usual, nothing happened at all. Dinner was seasoned with sparse, mundane conversation about the weather and the kids' upcoming sports events.

"Meatloaf tastes great, hon," I said.

She nodded and replied, "Lilly's soccer tournament starts next week."

"Yeah, I remember."

"Did you put in for time off?"

"I don't need to take time off for a game that starts at six p.m."

She frowned. "You know what I mean. Did you make arrangements to leave early, like I suggested? So you can actually get there on time for once. Maybe even help with a few things beforehand."

"No. There's no need to arrange anything. If my work is finished, I'll just leave early."

"I've heard that before."

We both sighed, and I took another bite of my suddenly bland meatloaf.

After dinner, we washed the dishes together in silence and then migrated to the living room to watch TV. Kate chose to sit in the armchair, leaving me stranded on our uncomfortably large couch. We stared in silence for a good hour before one of us finally spoke. "Did you get enough to eat?" she asked, her tone suddenly light and caring. I felt a spark of hope, and after a moment's consideration, I decided to join her in the armchair for some cuddle time. But before I could even leave my seat, she stood first and said, "I'm going to bed. I'm tired." And upstairs she went.

That was it. No goodnight. No kiss. I thought about it long after she had faded up the stairs—the unsettling spirit of a woman who was once much more alive than she is now.

When I entered the bedroom a half hour later, Kate was reading in bed. I took a minute to confer with my reflection in the bathroom mirror—something I often do when I'm nervous—pondering what I should say to her. I knew it needed to be good. Something interesting, exciting even, to break the tension and get us back on track. I couldn't allow the night to end in its current condition. There was a wave building, and I couldn't just sit back and wait for it to break over us. But what did she want to hear? How my day went? Recent accomplishments? Future goals? I felt like I was preparing for a job interview.

Eventually, I settled on a riveting announcement about paying this month's electric bill, which led to nothing more than an unimpressed nod from Kate. Then we lay in bed, silently entertaining ourselves—her with her e-reader and me with my phone. Before long, we were turning the lights off to go to sleep. Another day over.

At first, as I stared out into the darkness of the room, I was relieved. I had managed to avoid an argument, and I took that as a win. Soon enough, however, I realized I was cheering a rather shallow victory, and then my worries settled back into the pit of my stomach. All of the little issues that had been piling up and morphing into bigger problems would still be there in the morning, tapping their tiny feet against the hardwood floor. Singularly insignificant, perhaps, but the cumulative clamor had become ominous.

So today the uncomfortable distance remains, a distinct aura of tension that clouds the air with every breath.

On one hand, life is good. I've experienced success on many levels. I'm a senior-level engineer for one of the largest computer companies in the nation, and I own a four-bedroom home with a beautiful wife, and we have three amazing daughters. The American Dream all wrapped up into one neat, perfect package. So what's the problem?

Short answer: nothing, and everything.

Kate takes good care of me—she makes sure I'm fed and watered and get enough sunlight—but we don't see eye-to-eye on anything these days. She criticizes me for little things, like when I leave dishes in the sink, forget to pick up milk on my way home, or neglect to fix the leaky faucet. Communication has never been my strength, nor has memory.

Then there are the big, thunderous arguments. Our latest clash was over how she thought I spent too much money on a recent outing with a couple of guys from work. We hit up one of the local bars, drank beer, and enjoyed a few laughs. Anyone who knows me knows that I rarely have nights out like that. I should be allowed to go out and have fun once in a while without feeling bad about it. When I try to take her out somewhere—just the two of us—she almost always refuses. She'll say she's too tired or would rather save the money.

Kate has always had a fire in her. One thing she has always loved about me is my natural ability to calm that fire, to tamp the raging flame down to embers, for a little while at least. That ability doesn't come as easily as it used to, though. Which makes me wonder…when was the last time I perceived that fire as endearing and exciting, instead of just focusing on the severity of the burn?

***

I stand and stretch, clearing away the mental cobwebs of last night and jump into the shower. As I finish getting dressed for work, I'm startled by the sound of pans clanging together in the kitchen, and the scent of bacon wafting up the stairs. What is she doing home? She should have left for work over an hour ago. Perhaps she made arrangements to go in late so that we could have breakfast together. That would be a nice surprise.

CHAPTER THREE

BREAKFAST

I make my way downstairs to the kitchen and lean against the doorframe, feeling things out. Kate's not exactly a morning person, even when we *are* getting along.

She's facing the stove, wearing her favorite purple lion pajamas. Her hair is combed and styled, flowing down her back in thick brown waves.

I tiptoe through the room like a soldier picking his way through a minefield. Ridiculous, I know, but life doesn't supply us with a how-to manual on surviving interpersonal dilemmas such as these. So we do what we have to and tread lightly, hoping to find a solution somewhere along the way.

I place my hands on her arms and kiss her cheek. She leans into my lips—always a good sign.

"Good morning," I say.

"Good morning," she murmurs, as if daydreaming, unwilling to vacate a dream from last night that planted her far away. With a spatula gripped firmly in one hand, she shoves a pile of scrambled eggs back and forth inside her favorite cast-iron pan.

She's wearing makeup already, which strikes me as mildly disappointing. Her face is never more beautiful than when it's in its original, untouched state. All the makeup does is cover up what's already perfect.

I'm still attracted to her after all these years, and as far as I know, she feels the same about me. We're just too busy or exhausted to physically express those feelings most of the time. We've lost our spark. These days, that spark feels almost impossible to reach—a lost treasure buried deep in an underground labyrinth, safeguarded by seemingly endless booby traps and puzzles. Unfortunately, I'm no Indiana Jones, and she's no Lara Croft. Regardless, we'll need to dig deep if we want to keep this marriage alive.

"Have a seat," she says. "Breakfast is almost ready."

I glance at the bacon that's sizzling inside a separate pan before taking a seat at the table. I sit there quietly and wait—studying Kate's back as she continues to cook in silence like I'd never entered the room.

"How are you?" I ask.

"Fine."

"Sleep well?"

"Yup."

"That's good."

"Yup."

Well, we've exhausted that topic. I'd better come up with something more interesting to say before things take a turn for the worse.

"Running late for work?" I ask.

She spins around and glares at me, placing one hand on her hip. "I have an appointment this morning. Remember?"

"Oh, right," I say, feigning understanding, well aware that I've bumped a tripwire.

"Let me guess. You forgot, right?"

"No..." I race through the lanes and levels of my brain, moving down from cell to cell in the hopes of locating the exact moment when she revealed this small but vital tidbit of information. The memory is nowhere to be found. When I've combed through every level and finally reach the bottom floor, there's a white rabbit stretched out on a hammock by the ocean, wearing sunglasses and reading a book. "Don't look at *me*," he says. "I'm on vacation."

"I told you about it last week," she says.

"Yeah, I remember."

She shifts her weight and crosses her arms. "All right, then. What is the appointment for?" she asks, an edge of triumph in her voice.

"You know... To get checked out...and stuff. Doctor's appointment, right?"

She shakes her head. "Unbelievable. Do you ever listen when I talk? Or does your brain just shut off whenever the topic doesn't pertain to you, specifically?"

Any visions I had of a pleasant, leisurely conversation over breakfast are disappearing fast.

"Of course I do. It just slipped my mind, that's all. A lot happens during the week. I need reminders."

"Yes, I'm well aware."

My body goes rigid with tension.

She returns to the stove and pushes the eggs around some more. The pan slides and rattles against the hot metal coils. "I could use a reminder once in a while too, you know?" She lowers the heat and turns toward me. "When was the last time you reminded me about something?"

My mind draws a blank. Again.

"Something important, that is. The release date for the next Terminator movie doesn't count."

I let out a small gasp as my brain scrambles for an answer.

"Exactly," she says.

She paces the room like a lawyer about to give her closing arguments to the jury. "When you have appointments, I remember. When the girls have appointments, whether it be medical, dental, academic, sports, or otherwise... I remember. You know why I remember? Because it's important. And when something is important, I remember. So my question for you is..." She stops and looks me dead in the eye. "When will my needs be important enough to remember?"

I swallow, my tongue sticking for a moment to the roof of my dry mouth. "Hon, listen. I didn't forget entirely. I'm just not thinking clearly. It's still early. I haven't had any coffee yet."

"And another thing—" She steps over to the counter and presses the magic red button on our Keurig coffee maker. It starts to brew, filling the air with its distinct aroma. "Don't you think I would have left for work already if I didn't have somewhere else to be first? That should have triggered something right away."

"It did trigger...something."

"And what was that?"

"That you were running late, or possibly not going to work at all."

She dips her head forward, awaiting more information.

"Just because..." I continue.

"Just because..." Her echo is dry, somewhere between incredulity and resignation. She holds her chin with one hand and nods. "We both know I never skip work or run late, *just because.*"

I'm starting to reach my limit for being told what I should already know. "Do you have to speak to me like I'm a suspect in a criminal investigation?"

She tosses her hands up. "I'm sorry. I guess I just don't know any other way to talk to you these days. When I speak nicely, you either don't hear me, or you forget what I say."

"Whatever you say, dear."

With that, an intense staring contest begins. She's usually the first to break it with one biting comment or another, but for once a decent comeback strikes me first.

"I also thought you may have stayed home to have breakfast with me. Silly me. I'll never make that mistake again."

"Don't try to turn this around and make me feel bad. It's not going to work in your favor."

I raise my hands in the air, palms out. "All right, you've made your point. Jesus, I was just making small talk."

"Ron, small talk is the only form of communication we've had for weeks. It's literally killing me." She holds two fists in the air for emphasis.

I close my eyes and take a couple of deep breaths. "Okay, I get it, and I'm sorry. Now would you relax, please?"

"I *was* perfectly relaxed before you came down here and started asking me stupid questions."

The bacon pops.

"I understand," I say. "Again, I'm sorry."

She flips the bacon, then stands there quietly for a moment, massaging her forehead. "No... *I'm* sorry. I shouldn't snap at you like that." She turns to face me. "It's just... We never talk anymore, and I feel extremely alone."

"But why, for God's sake? You're only alone for two hours a day."

She closes her eyes, squeezing her eyelids together so tight that I can only assume she's trying to push my words back out of her ears. "I need more time with you, Ron." She opens her eyes, and I sense a pleading note in her voice that I hadn't noticed before. "That's all I'm saying. And I never get it during the week because you're either away from home or burnt out from work and your commute. Which is fine. I get it. I have to. But I also have my limits." She gazes at me with desperate, bloodshot eyes, searching for something I can only assume I lack. With her cheeks now pink and swollen, she appears younger and more vulnerable, like she did in the early years of our marriage, when every disagreement served to remind us just how much we loved each other, when they led to actual resolutions instead of lingering trails of resentment.

Noise emerges from the Keurig as it finishes brewing, spewing liquid like blood from a head wound.

Kate glances at the coffee crime scene. "I didn't marry you so we would never talk to each other. I shouldn't feel lonely. Hell, even when we're together, I feel alone. Do you know that? Do you know why that is?"

I shake my head.

"Because you and I spend time alone, together. Think about that for a moment."

I let the words sink in: *alone, together*. The oxymoron bumps and grinds its way through my brain as I try to relate it to how she's feeling. I picture us in the evenings, concentrating on everything but each other. The kids, the dishes, the laundry. Preparing for the next day. Watching TV, reading, sleeping. I get what she's saying, but I've always assumed that's how most couples in America spend their evenings, especially if they've been married for ten-plus years and have multiple kids. Still, I doubt that will pass as an acceptable defense.

"It's messed up, right?" she asks.

I nod. "It really is."

"I shouldn't feel this way." She grabs the mug of coffee, adds cream and sugar to it and stirs. "And now, with the girls away for the rest of the week, it's the perfect opportunity for us to sit and have a real conversation. Clear the air a bit. Reconnect. But instead, you seem perfectly content saying nothing at all. I don't think you said more than ten words to me last night after the girls left. You were more than happy just staring at your phone until we fell asleep."

"I was just tired. I needed to zone out on something meaningless for a while."

She blinks at me, which tells me she's still waiting to hear a valid reason for my behavior. Kate's a professional blinker. She can convey almost any thought or feeling with just her eyelids. "And what about you?" I say. "You did the same thing."

"I was waiting for *you* to talk."

"Okay, but, you didn't have to. You could have said *something*."

She nods. "You're right, I could have. And I probably should have. But I really wanted you to take the lead for once. I *needed* you to take the lead, Ron. Plus, I figured, if you wanted to talk to me, then you would have. But you didn't, thinking about God knows what instead, leaving me to wonder. Meanwhile, I'm left with a million things still running through my mind and nowhere to put it all." She sets the mug down on the table in front of me.

"Thank you." I take my first sip of coffee, while she stares at me with pleading eyes that desperately try to reiterate all of her previous sentiments.

"Do you see where I'm coming from, at least?" she implores.

I sip my coffee again, louder than intended. "Yes."

"Any thoughts of your own you'd like to share?"

I take a moment to collect my thoughts with the help of caffeine and the much-needed clarity it brings, then I look her right in the eye. "I honestly had no idea that you were keeping all of this inside," I say.

A thoughtful frown joins her eyebrows together. I want to hug her and reassure her that everything will be fine. Better than fine. I want my embrace to have the power to eliminate the weight of so many small, heavy burdens. But I fear she'll only interpret the gesture as an attempt at avoiding the conversation.

I glance up and notice that the top button of her pajama shirt is undone, exposing the small, exciting alleyway that runs between her breasts. Suddenly, that's all I can think about as I steer my eyes down along her body, studying the way her pajamas cling to every curve.

I set the mug down and smirk. "Come here."

She crosses her arms defiantly. "No."

The bacon pops again. Grease shoots out and sizzles against the counter.

"Please?"

She lets out a small but dramatic sigh and sits on my lap. I wrap my arms around her and give her a tender kiss. Whenever we kiss, I'm able to travel back in time to when we first met and fell in love. All of the tastes, smells, and textures come racing back through my mind. Her apple-scented shampoo. The lilacs outside her front door. The softness of her skin under a bright summer sun...

I try to look her in the eye, but she's staring off to the side, toward the floor.

"Kate, honey. Look at me." She finally allows her gaze to connect with mine. "I *do* see where you're coming from," I say. "And now that I know, I promise I'll do better."

She shakes her head slowly. Her beautiful smile finally appears, then simmers back down. "I wish I could believe you, Ron. I really do. But I've heard all this from you before. You always say the right things after the fact, when you don't want me to stay mad at you."

"And I always mean them."

"But then nothing changes!"

I huff, annoyed and unsure of where this leaves us, or what she wants me to do. All I know is that I miss her. Especially right now, as I sit here, holding her close to me, staring into those big brown eyes of hers.

"It's fine," she says, the momentary smile flattening again. "Just let me know when you can free up enough time in your busy schedule to have a real conversation with me."

She stares at the floor again, avoiding my gaze. After a few seconds, she attempts to wiggle away and escape, but I maintain a firm grip. Her eyes return to me. A slight smile flickers at the corners of her lips. "You aren't going to get a pass by acting cute."

"I'm not?" I ask.

"No. It's too late for that." I know she means it, but again, it's her smile that reassures me she's still within my grasp. This battle isn't over yet.

"It's too late, huh?" I ask.

"That's right."

"Well, in that case, I might as well start searching for a new wife. Someone who *will* give me a pass and let me hold her after I apologize."

She scowls, then quickly composes herself, fixing her confident expression on me. "Do what you want. It occurred to me recently that you may have already found someone else."

"Really?"

"Really."

"And why on Earth would that occur to you?"

She shrugs. "I don't know... You're so disinterested in me these days, I figure you must be getting attention elsewhere."

I tilt my head, disappointed in her for even thinking it. "Hardly."

"And with those long, hard work hours of yours... Gone all the time..."

"Very funny. I hope that's not really what you think, because it's far from the truth. And I'm not disinterested in you. Quite the opposite, in fact." I move my eyebrows up and down a few times.

She snorts and rolls her eyes. "Whatever you say."

I lift her left hand and kiss the top of it, above her wedding ring.

She touches the side of my face with her right hand. My heart swells in my chest. "I love you, Kate."

"I love you, too."

"I need you."

"Really?" She says it like she doesn't believe me.

I lean in to give her a kiss but she pushes me back, raising her chin in an arrogant manner. "I don't believe you."

"Then I'll just have to prove it to you," I say, massaging her legs with my hands, starting just above her knees and gradually working my way up her thighs. Her eyes close, and her breathing becomes sensual. I kiss her neck. She shifts restlessly in my lap like she's tingling.

"Let's go upstairs," I whisper, then kiss her lips softly.

"What for?" she murmurs against my lips. Her words flow directly from her mouth to mine and down inside my lungs. They sting like smoke. She kisses me back.

I move my hands underneath her shirt and up the small of her back where her skin is extra sensitive. She arches back, then leans forwards against me. Her chest melts into mine. I kiss her cheek, then her neck again. "You know…"

"You wish." Her warm breath splashes against my ear. I won't give up that easily.

The tight space between her shirt and her back becomes frustrating, so I bring my hands forward and begin unbuttoning her top. Her face burns red—a small flame appearing on each cheekbone as I work my way down. She does nothing to halt my progress. I bring my lips to her chest. My hands are now able to move freely along every inch of her back, my fingers tracing the dips and hollows beneath her smooth, soft skin. Her eyes roll back and close, and her breathing deepens.

"I can be a little late for work," I say, kissing her warm cheek. With her eyes still closed, she wraps her arms around me, spearing her hands through my hair. I can't take much more of this. I need more of her. I bring one hand forward, toward her chest, but she grabs my wrist and pulls it right back to its starting point. "Come on," I say. "What's the matter? It's been so long."

She opens her eyes and leans back a little.

"What?" I ask.

A mini explosion of grease erupts behind her, and the smell of burnt bacon begins to permeate the air.

She grabs both sides of her shirt and thrusts them back together like a stage curtain, announcing loud and clear that this particular show is over. She pushes each button back through its hole, even the one at the very top.

"What's wrong?"

"Nothing. I need to get back to the stove." Her tone has changed again. Her forehead is now wrinkled with seriousness, and all traces of humor have drained from her face.

I stare at her with frustrated blankness, still holding her tight in my arms.

"No, really," she says. "The food is literally burning."

I glance behind her and see smoke rising from the pan. She retreats to the stove, working fast to fix the mess.

"I obviously did something wrong," I say.

The smoke alarm goes off.

I squeeze my hands into tight fists and stand, shoving my chair against the wall. I walk over and wave my hand back and forth beneath the smoke detector to shut it up. Once the shrieking stops, I drop my body back down on the chair. "What did I say to make you switch gears so fast?"

"Just go to work, Ron. Maybe we can try again tonight."

"Sure," I say, sulking.

"And since you can be so late for work, how about you wash these dishes before you go? Get some laundry started."

"Why are you being so unreasonable?"

She turns toward me, soaking up my annoyance with hard, scornful eyes. "Unreasonable?"

Oops...

"How, exactly, am I being unreasonable? Because I don't want to have a quickie with you here in the kitchen while the house burns down around us? Or because I suggested you do something that I do every single day—without an ounce of appreciation?"

"Let me rephrase…"

"Yeah, how about you do that." She turns the burners off on the stove.

"You're home by noon every day. It makes more sense for you to handle the dishes."

"And I do. Every day."

"And also just the way you said it was…shitty and unreasonable."

She nods.

"It's not like I sit on my ass when I get home at night, watching television and drinking beer until I fall asleep. I help around the house and with the girls. That's more than I can say for most men I know."

"Really? You're gonna pull that card? Because that doesn't impress me at all, Ron. I don't give a shit what other men do."

"Okay, but—"

"That's like me saying you're an amazing husband just because you don't beat me or degrade me."

I take a small breath and rethink my words. "I'm just saying you have a tendency to act like I have an easygoing job that requires minimal effort, and I can just come and go whenever I please."

"No, I don't. I'm simply saying that when two people agree to get married, buy an expensive home, and raise three kids together, there's a lot to do. And you leave most of it to me. And sometimes I can't handle it all. But that's not even what gets to me—because like you said, I work fewer hours than you, so it makes sense that I do more around the house. I'm not arguing that. What gets to me is how easily you take me for granted."

"How do you figure?" I ask.

She tosses her hand in the air. "God, where to begin… You never help with laundry unless I point out the thirty-foot pile of dirty clothes that's been building for a week. Dirty dishes will grow mold before you'll even consider moving them from the sink to the dishwasher or, God forbid, wash them yourself. Our sliding door would still be broken if I hadn't nagged you about it for weeks."

"Well, in my defense—"

"Nothing productive ever gets done unless I beg or do it myself."

"During the week, maybe. But the weekend is different. You can't tell me that I don't contribute to anything on the weekends."

"You do, yes. Here and there, in between extended sessions of relaxation and playtime with the girls."

I close my eyes and rub my fingers hard against my eyelids.

"Evelyn is old enough to help around the house now. Or even Lilly, for that matter. It wouldn't kill them to learn some responsibility, you know? But I know you would never ask them to lift a finger. I have to handle that as well, which makes me the evil parent and the bitch wife. Lucky me."

"The girls are still young," I say.

"They're not that young anymore, Ron. Hell, Olivia helps me more than the rest of you put together, and she's only three."

"Yeah, because she's your clone…" I mumble under my breath.

"Excuse me?"

"Nothing…"

Kate blinks a few times to express her annoyance.

I rub my chin. "I'm always more than happy to do whatever you ask of me."

"You're missing the point, entirely. I don't want to *have* to ask you to do things. I want you to just be aware, and notice on your own, and then do it. Then it's one less thing I have to think about."

"I'm sorry if I don't notice things the way you do. It's not my fault you have a special talent for finding work to do."

"Yeah, that's what it is. Really, Ron?"

"All right, I'm sorry. That was a stupid thing to say."

"Uh-huh."

"Does it really take that much effort for you to ask me to do something?"

"Yes!" she yells. "It's exhausting!"

"More exhausting than doing it?"

"Yes!"

"Well, I can't relate to that at all," I say. "I'd much rather tell people what to do than do it myself. Why do you think people become managers? So they can task others instead of doing the work themselves!"

"Ah, so by that logic, what you're telling me is that I'm the boss in this relationship, and you're my employee. Do I have that right?"

"Well…"

She shakes her head. "Not sexy, Ron. And not what I signed up for. I signed up for a marriage of equals—not for a second job overseeing a man-child." She heads back to the stove. "And you wonder why we're not having hot, flaming sex on top of the kitchen table right now."

"I never suggested… Look, let's take a step back here. I admit, I'm not the best at expressing appreciation."

Kate laughs.

"But, I do appreciate you. I promise. I thank you all the time for everything you do."

She looks at her feet and nods. "Mm-hmm."

"And I think I help plenty. Even on the weeknights."

"You have fun with the girls, Ron. You play games and goof around."

"What's wrong with that?"

She steps toward me, jerking her hands forward. "Nothing! I love that you enjoy the kids so much and that they adore you. It's one of the reasons I married you. One of the reasons I stay married to you. But it's not enough. It's not fair that I have to handle all of the discipline, all of the school stuff, all of the appointments, all the errands, all the groceries…" She places her hand on her forehead. "Jesus, don't get me started on the fucking groceries."

"All right…" I say.

"FYI, just in case you aren't aware, I hate buying groceries!" she yells.

"Got it." I won't argue that one. Grocery stores are the worst.

"I spare you from having to deal with it because it *sucks*, but it would be nice if you came with me once in a while."

"Okay. I can do that."

She takes a deep breath and resets. "I spend every evening cooking, cleaning, helping the girls with homework, making sure they are bathed and ready for school the next day, and then," she continues in a constricted, loud voice, "you come home just in time to entertain them and make them laugh for an hour before they go to sleep."

I can hear the blood pounding in my ears, and the words spewing from my mouth aren't bothering to check in with my brain before they go. "I work those long hours in order to provide for this family. So you can be home with the girls instead of missing out on half their childhoods like I am. That's what you wanted, remember? I made that happen for you. Not for *me*. For *you*."

"All right," she says, holding her hand up in protest. "You've made your point."

"And I'll be damned if I'm going to come home and spend the one hour I get with them telling them to do chores."

"All right!" she yells.

"Congratulations on being the first woman to be annoyed with her husband for enjoying his children too much."

"Are you done?" Her voice is level now, and I realize that I've been speaking just as loud as she was. She turns her back to me, scraping the bacon off the pan and grabbing a couple of plates from the cabinet.

My hands are shaking. "I don't know why you insist on arguing with me first thing in the goddamn morning. Why can't we just sit down and have a nice breakfast together like a normal married couple?"

She smirks, ever-so-slightly. "Is that what normal married couples do, Ron?"

"Yes. I believe it is."

She nods. "How enlightening. I had no idea. Why didn't you tell me this sooner?"

I sigh.

"What else do they do together?" she asks. She jaunts over and leans her hands against the table next to me. "Let me guess. I bet they have sex too, don't they?"

"Forget it, Kate."

"No, please." She pulls out a chair and sits beside me. "Educate me on the activities of normal married couples, since you're obviously an expert on the subject."

I throw my hands up. "That's all I've got. Sorry."

She nods. "Too bad."

Kate heads back to the stove and scoops food from the pan to the plates and pours two cups of orange juice.

"I'll tell you what, Ron. What do you say we go ahead and try it anyway?" she asks, her voice oozing with an edginess that makes my entire body ache like I've been driving a car for ten hours straight. "I'll wear my best smile and treat you like a king. That way we can continue to leave all of our problems on the back burner and pretend everything is fine." She sets a plate of food and a cup of juice down in front of me and then sits down on the other side of the table with her own. "Sound good?" She flashes a cheesy, insincere grin and takes a big bite of her eggs. The bacon is so burnt that it's actually black.

"Yeah, great."

"Good."

"Because everything should be good, damn it."

"Should it?"

"Yes! Sure, there are things we need to work on, but something's got to give here. I can't even concentrate at work half the time because I'm too busy stressing about this shit."

Kate breaks off a small piece of bacon and eats it, nodding vaguely like I'm talking about the weather. It crunches between her teeth like a potato chip.

I take a breath. "I don't need to be treated like a king," I continue. "I work hard. You work hard. Marriage and jobs and raising kids is stressful. That's just life."

"Well, thank you for that brilliant insight, dear. I can feel the loneliness withering away already."

"The key is to not take it out on each other. We have to find a way to discuss these things like mature adults. If we can do that, then I think we'll be fine."

She nods again, chewing her charcoal bacon chips. "Mm-hm."

"I wouldn't be surprised if Abby and Tim next door are having this same conversation right now."

"They could very well be," she says, appearing semi-convinced. Is it possible I'm getting through to her?

"And there's probably nothing wrong with their marriage either. They're fine. Just like we're fine."

"You're right."

"I am? You agree?"

"Absolutely," she says. "It's just adulthood, and we all have to deal with it."

"Exactly."

"I just need to accept things the way they are and count my blessings."

"There you go," I say. "I think that's the best way to look at it. You'll feel better if you do, trust me." I grab my fork and take a bite of my eggs, which have a rubbery, overcooked texture.

"That's certainly one way to minimize my feelings."

I stop chewing. An audible clank echoes through the room as I drop my fork back down onto my plate.

She continues eating. I clench my fists, frustrated. Not only with her and this entire argument, but with myself for never knowing the right thing to say.

My voice is dry and void of emotion. "I'm just trying to keep my head above water here. Usually, when you're irritated with me, I don't even know why. Half the time, I don't even know there's a problem until you're blowing up at me. That's why I don't have much to say while you're quietly waiting for me to 'take the lead' and fix everything by saying all the right words."

She keeps the fake grin turned up full beam. "There isn't a problem, Ron. No problem at all. Everything's fine. It's just me being crazy and irrational, as usual. You don't need to change a thing." She stabs the eggs with her fork. "You're perfect just the way you are—"

"Enough!" I slam my fist down hard on the table. The impact causes her spoon to bounce off the table and land on the floor. Juice splashes up from her cup and spills on her eggs.

She stares down at her plate with glistening eyes, and my anger washes away. Now all I want is to give her a hug.

I pick her spoon up off the floor, wipe it with a napkin, and set it back down on the table. I lean in and gently kiss her forehead, which is warm and damp like she's purging her resentment through her pores.

"I'm sorry, hon."

"It's fine," she says. "The food is awful, anyway." She shoves her plate away from her. "Sorry I ruined breakfast."

I sit back down in my chair. "I'm not trying to put our problems off. I'm a simple man, Kate. I just want to sit here and enjoy breakfast with you before I go to work. Is that too much to ask?"

She shakes her head, still staring at her plate. "Nope."

"I got an idea, why don't we start the morning over. Pretend that we're a different couple entirely. A couple that doesn't argue with each other. What do you say? It'll be fun. Like roleplaying, minus the kinky aspect."

She remains silent.

"Or maybe I'll just finish eating and leave." I grab my fork. "We'll talk more tonight after work."

"Unless, of course, you're too tired." Her voice is low and muted.

I put the fork back down. "You know what? You win. I never should have even walked in here, I should have just gone straight to work. I'm out of here. Have a great day." And with that I get up and walk into the hall to put on my light tan-colored jacket and grab my bag off the floor. "I don't know why I even try," I say loud enough for her to hear me.

"Me neither," she replies so quietly I'm not sure she meant for me to hear it.

I walk back down the hall and observe her from the kitchen doorway. She hasn't moved. She's staring at the spilled juice, tears rolling down her cheeks. She sniffs a couple of times, and my chest tightens. Whenever she cries, my insides start to twist and turn, like my guts are trying to form a knot. I can't leave this way. I'm mad, but I don't want her to be sad.

I walk back into the kitchen and approach her. "Will you at least tell me what you made the appointment for? If you don't, I'm just going to worry about it all day."

"It's nothing you need to be concerned about," she responds, maintaining her hushed tone. "I'm just going to talk to someone."

"Talk to who? Your doctor? It's a medical appointment, right?"

"Sort of."

"Sort of? What does that mean?"

"I mean it's not my usual doctor."

"Who then?"

She doesn't respond.

"Like a therapist?"

She looks me in the eye. "To be honest, I'm not at liberty to discuss the details of it with you."

I place my hands on my hips. "Really?"

She lets out a nervous breath. "It's nothing. It's just someone who's been very successful with helping people work through their anxiety, using various…unique methods. Now will you please go to work and stop interrogating me?"

"Anxiety? I didn't realize it was that bad. Helping people how? Prescription meds to dope you up and turn you into a zombie?"

"I don't know. I haven't gone yet."

I tilt my head and frown. Her eyes return to the table.

"Kate…" I step closer to her.

"I'm hurting, Ron."

I rest my hand on her shoulder. "Sweetie… You don't need that stuff."

"I think maybe I do."

"What if it changes you?"

"That's kind of the point."

"You know what I mean. What if it makes you feel worse?"

Her eyes peer up at me, sharp and direct. "I can't imagine feeling worse than I do right now."

My heart weighs heavily in my chest. I lean in and attempt a goodbye hug.

She shifts her body away. "Don't."

I bite my tongue.

It's official; I don't enjoy being married anymore. What's the point if I'm not even allowed to hug my own wife? Hugging has always been one of our things. A way to express our deep love for one another, especially when our words fail us. We used to say how perfectly we blend together, then add the additional side joke: "Even more so with our clothes off." Hell, she hugged me the day we met. But standing here now in this kitchen, staring down at her, her body tense and full of anger... She might as well be a stranger.

I step out of the house, tempted to slam the front door just to make a point, to emphasize my anger. I hesitate before closing it, adding more weight to the decision than it deserves. As if this one minuscule choice could change what I find on the other side. I consider all of this and close the door soundlessly behind me.

CHAPTER FOUR

THE BOOKSTORE, 1989

The first time I met Kate, it was a hot summer's day inside a used bookstore on 3rd Avenue. We were still young—eighteen and some change. I was fresh out of high school and still living in my parents' basement, trying to decide what to do with my life. The store was small but perfect for finding old, rare books. I walked in and headed back toward the classics, as always.

On that particular day, though, someone was in my way. She was standing in the narrow aisle, browsing the history shelf. There was a minimal amount of space between shelves, and as I turned my body sideways to try to slide past her, she stepped back and walked right into me.

"Oh," we both said in unison as she whipped around to face me. Only, the tone of my "oh" sounded more like "oops" and the tone of hers was more like "oh my."

Her wide, curious eyes met mine.

"Excuse *you*," she said with more than a hint of attitude, her words quickly turning the moment sour.

I made a face, unimpressed. "My bad."

She wrinkled her nose at me. "*My bad*? What does that even mean? Who says that?"

I shrugged. "I do, obviously. And it means that I'm apologizing." We stared at each other as if we were both aliens, offended that we'd landed on the same planet. I was ready to move on. "Well, take care. Sorry again."

I turned to walk away, but her voice reeled me back in. "Are you really, though?" she asked.

I stopped and looked at her. "Pardon?"

"Are you really sorry?"

"Yeah. Why would I say I was if I wasn't?" I suddenly felt stupid, like I was missing something obvious.

"Because you didn't sound sincere, that's why. And also, when a guy walks over and thrusts his..." she glanced at my crotch "...pubic bone against my ass, I assume it's on purpose."

"Pubic bone?"

She lifted her chin. "That's right."

"Who says that?"

She combed her fingers through her hair and looked rather pretty doing it. "I do, obviously."

"I think you mean pelvic bone."

The redness of her cheeks intensified as she scanned my face with her eyes. "What's the difference?"

"Well..." I had no clue. "I don't know. But I know there is one."

"Are they close together, at least?" she asked, pointing at my crotch.

I shifted my weight and felt the heat inside my ears. "Yes. I'm ninety-five percent sure."

She raised her eyebrows, unconvinced. "Fascinating. Are you a doctor?"

"No."

"What are you, then?"

"Uh…" I scratched my head. "I'm not anything. Not yet, anyways. But I'm thinking about going to school for computers. You know, IT stuff."

Her stern confidence began to fade. "Hmm… I'm not anything yet, either. Just a waitress, working at The Satellite."

"The Satellite?" I asked.

"Yeah. It's a restaurant on Broadway Street. They've got little stars and planets all over the walls. It's pretty cool." She nodded to herself. "You've never been there?"

I shook my head, suddenly mesmerized. "Can't say I have."

"You're missing out. Their buffalo wings are to die for."

"Are they?" I said.

"And supposably their chicken quesadillas are pretty rock-n-roll too, but I haven't tried them yet."

"Supposably?" I repeated with a smirk. "You mean supposedly?"

She smiled shyly and looked down like she was embarrassed.

"It sounds great," I said. "Really."

She peered up at me. "You should come by sometime."

"You're right. I should."

She lifted her head and smiled again. "Awesome. I work every day but Thursday and Sunday. Nights."

"Got it."

She bit down on the corner of her bottom lip and nodded, glancing around the room briefly. "So, computers, huh?"

"Yeah…" I glanced down at my feet.

"Cool."

I shrugged. "Occasionally."

She gave me a crooked grin like she understood and appreciated the joke. I couldn't help but smile back.

"Anyway," I said, returning to the topic at hand and doing my best to hide my smile, "just for the record, *you* hit *me* with your ass." I pointed at her behind. "Not the other way around. I was just passing by, minding my own business."

She reached up as if to touch me, and plucked a loose hair off my shoulder. "Is that what you're telling yourself?"

"Well, yeah. I mean, no. It's just the truth."

"Do you always tell the truth?"

"Are you always this aggressive?"

She flashed a mischievous smirk. "Got any more gum?"

I had forgotten I was even chewing gum.

"Uh… Yeah…" I dug down into my pocket and pulled out my pack. She held her hand out, and I pushed a piece through the foil and into her hand.

She placed it on the tip of her tongue, and in the time that it took me to blink, the gum had disappeared. "Thanks a bunch."

"No sweat."

"I'm Kate."

"Ron."

We talked for a while, probably louder than we should have, but I didn't care. It wasn't long before I found myself leaning closer to her, taking in every word like oxygen, my eyes tracking her every move, eager to hear what she would say next. I started noticing details about her appearance that my mind had skipped past earlier. The little yellow lion on her t-shirt. How her toenail polish matched her sandals perfectly, both purple with white polka dots. How soft her legs looked, and how her slightly-too-tight denim shorts accentuated her butt.

We spent a few more minutes discussing books and other common interests, such as cliff jumping, using the word "fascinating" sarcastically, and scaring people when they're in the shower. I only found that last one mildly amusing, whereas she seemed to get some sort of deep emotional fulfillment out of it. I also learned that she hated nuts on her ice cream unless it was chocolate ice cream—then, it was okay. And people who back into parking spaces instead of just pulling in—as if they're "above all that driving in reverse business." That drove her crazy.

It crossed my mind to mention how both options require driving in reverse and that it was just a matter of when. But I decided there was no point. It wasn't going to change how she felt.

Eventually, she announced that she had to go. She wrote her number on a purple sticky note and handed it to me. I thanked her, and our eyes wandered around each other, nervously looking for a proper spot to rest. I couldn't keep my gaze from sliding back and forth across her face, trying to take in her every feature. She was a new, vibrant color in what I had thought was a monochrome world.

I leaned forward and kissed her cheek. It felt warm and soft against my lips. I hadn't planned on doing it; it just happened. Her hand touched my face for the briefest of moments until I pulled away.

I looked at her, feeling as though I'd been struck by a jolt of electricity. Something had changed in her eyes. They appeared more precious than before. More vulnerable. She pursed her lips and closed the short space between us by giving me a strong, heartfelt hug. My heart fluttered against my ribs as it tried to get closer to her.

After she left, I read the note. Next to the number, she'd written, "Call me—maybe we can bump pubic bones again sometime."

I drove home with a massive smile painted across my face, listening to bouncy pop music and singing along at the top of my lungs, with no concern for how stupid I looked.

CHAPTER FIVE

THE ACCIDENT

When I start my car, a loud burst of angry words and heavy guitar riffs explode from the speakers, giving me an uncomfortable shock. I've had the same rock CD stuck in the stereo for months, and due to what I can only assume is loose wiring, the music blasts at full volume whenever I turn on the car. Usually I only find it mildly annoying or embarrassing, depending on the time and place, but right now it's perfect fuel for my fire.

I don't signal as I back out of my driveway. I don't even bother to put my seatbelt on. I blaze down the road in my orange 1974 Toyota Corolla. Everyone I know hates my car because of its color and age. Kate, in particular, loves to push my buttons by claiming it looks more peach than orange.

Kate. Her name feeds into my anger, tinting the edges of my vision and weighing my foot down on the gas pedal. I lean forward and scream at the windshield, harsh and wordless, drowning out the music for a few short moments. The rearview and side mirrors vibrate in time with the bass. I punch the padded roof above me several times, my knuckles leaving shallow indents in their wake.

I spot a woman jogging along the street, coming toward me in the opposite direction. I see her almost every morning on my way to work, wearing a tank top and black running shorts, her brown hair in a ponytail, swaying back and forth as she runs. She always smiles at me as I drive past her, and I always wave and smile back. I don't have it in me to smile right now, so I step on the gas and continue past her without looking.

I stop at a red light and wait. Kate's heavy black coat occupies the seat next to me. I eye it bitterly. The man in the car behind me honks his horn because the light is green.

Moving forward and picking up speed, I grip the steering wheel and imagine swerving straight into the oncoming traffic and exploding into a burst of flames. Wouldn't be the worst way to go.

Thrashing guitars scream through the speakers, and I scream along with it. "God, what is her problem?" I yell. "Why can't she let up for one goddamn second?"

Our anniversary.

I'm surprised she didn't mention it earlier. Has it not been on her mind? Or is she testing me? Waiting to see if I remember on my own. It's possible she forgot, but I doubt it. I'll stop and get her something on my way home from work tonight. Then I can give it to her in the morning. If I even see her, that is. Or I could just say "screw it," since we're on the verge of divorce anyway.

All the houses, lawns, and apartment buildings blur past the windows of my little boxed-off world. I press down harder on the gas, squeezing the steering wheel and feeling the blood drain from my hands. Traffic lights zoom past me in ribbons of color as I fly through each intersection. I just want things to be the way they were. When we were happy. My eyes well with tears as I picture my daughters' sweet little faces.

There's a black dot moving across the street ahead. I blink to clear my eyes, and the dot forms the shape of a cat, trying to cross the road—but it's not moving fast enough. The cat freezes, unsure of where to go. Panic sets in. My scattered mind is suddenly clear and sharp: take the cat's life or risk my own to avoid it. I whip the steering wheel to the right, practically grazing a car in the next lane. Car horns are sounding off all around me. I whip the steering wheel left. The tires screech and burn. The car jumps the curb with a violent thump, landing me on an island of grass. I push down on the brake as hard as I can, but the car slides sideways, spinning and screeching, and then stopping violently with a crash. The impact rips my body from the seat, and my head cracks against the unforgiving rearview mirror above.

Dazed, I lean against the steering wheel, wincing in pain as the music lances through my brain. I manage to move my arms—not broken, thank God—and turn the volume down on the stereo. My heart pounds against my throat.

I pull the door handle, but it won't budge. There's a stop sign lodged in the door. I sit up straight, shift into reverse, and back away from the sign. A loud scraping noise screeches and echoes through the air, and I flinch as it fuels the pain in my head.

I pull the handle again, and the door swings open with a loud squeak. I slip my legs out, reaching upwards to feel for the painful lump, which is located on the upper right-hand corner of my forehead. The pounding in my head quickly becomes unbearable, moving first through my temples, then swirling through my skull. A breeze blows through and embraces me, giving me the chills.

The black cat emerges from the front of the car and approaches me. It stops a couple of feet away and stares.

"What are you looking at?" I say. "See what you did?" I gesture toward the car with my hand. "My day was already shitty enough without your help." It keeps staring at me with the same bored expression. I sigh. "Thanks for nothing."

The cat blinks a couple times, then winds itself between my legs and purrs. I reach down and pet it, trying to ignore the rush of nausea that comes from changing positions. The cat seems grateful for the attention. No collar or identification. Someone in a white pickup truck pulls up over the grass and parks behind my car. The cat runs away—its tail shooting straight up and bristling. It successfully makes its way across the street and disappears into the bushes.

A clean-cut, handsome young man with dirty blonde hair steps out of the truck, wearing jeans and a plain navy blue t-shirt. "Hey, mister. Are you okay?" He speaks with a slight accent, but I'll be damned if I know where it's from.

I exhale all the air from my lungs. "Depends on what you mean by 'okay.'"

The young man hesitates. "Sir, are you hurt?"

"No, I'm fine. I appreciate the concern, though."

"But, sir, you're bleeding." He reaches up and touches his forehead. I do the same, pressing my fingers to the lump, then observing the blood on my fingertips. "Damn, I guess you're right." I look at him. "It's nothing, though, really. Just a scratch."

"You sure? I could call an ambulance, if you like."

"No, no." I wave my hand in objection. "I'll be fine, honestly."

"Well, all right then. If you're sure." He hesitates again. "Do you mind if I ask what happened?"

I toss my hand in the air. "Goddamn cat ran in the road. I was trying not to kill it."

"I see. So there were no other cars involved?"

"Nope. Just mine."

"Well that's good, at least." He climbs back into his truck and puts his seatbelt on. "You be careful now, mister. I'd have that looked at if I were you."

"Thanks. You're a very well-mannered young man. Your parents obviously did something right."

"Thanks. They did all right, I suppose."

"You got a girlfriend? Or a wife?"

"Yeah. Girlfriend."

"Good for you. How's that working out?"

"Well... Boyfriend, actually."

I smile and nod.

"It's working out fine," he says.

"Good. You guys get along well?"

"Yeah. Most of the time."

"Probably not too much drama, when it's two guys, huh?"

"You'd be surprised. We have our fair share, believe me."

I stare down at the grass, lost in thought. "Yeah, I suppose so." I think of Kate for a moment and my vision blurs—a deep sea of green. My eyes water.

"Mister, you sure you're gonna be okay?"

I regain focus. "Positive," I say, standing up to approach the truck. I extend my hand. "Thanks again. I'm Ron."

He shakes my hand with a firm grip. "Casey."

"Good to meet you, Casey."

His eyes are a striking light blue. He's got a small scar below his left eye.

"You too, Ron. I hope everything works out for you."

He pulls back onto the highway and disappears around the next curve. It's good to know there are still honest, caring strangers in the world.

I take a moment to examine the large dent on my driver's side door. How am I going to explain that to Kate?

I get in my car and drive away. Thankfully, it still runs fine.

I observe a man sprinting alongside the road. He's buff and sweaty. I envy his dedication to fitness and better health. The jogging woman re-enters my mind. I shouldn't have ignored her earlier. It's not her fault my morning's been awful.

I recall the one time I spoke to her...

One evening, I left the house to go for a walk. I needed to cool down and get some fresh air after arguing with Kate. She was coming toward me, walking her large golden retriever on a leash. The dog had stopped to sniff the ground and contemplate the best spot to do its business when I finally reached her. She appeared to be in her late thirties, early forties. In great shape. Pretty. She said hello and we chatted briefly. Her voice had a light southern drawl to it that I found both pleasant and relaxing. She also had these amazing brown eyes. A bit lighter than her hair. They seemed to glow at times. I imagine more than a few men have found themselves lost inside of them.

Recently divorced, she lives alone. "Finally free." She was a couple of inches shorter than me and had a way of looking up at me through her eyelashes. She also had a deadly flair for sarcasm. "Sarcasm and I get along well," she told me. She was confident and cool, like she had it all figured out. Though I suspected that in her mind, it was quite the opposite.

I didn't learn much else about her that day, but she certainly left her mark, as attractive, outgoing women with lively spirits tend to do. But there was much more to her than that. I could tell immediately that she was interesting and fun. She'd been places. Experienced things. She was someone who left sparks of joy in others wherever she went, despite a few minor traces of sadness I caught hiding within her face. Someone I'd enjoy being friends with. Is such a thing even possible?

Oddly enough, she never told me her name. And I forgot to tell her mine. She did, however, introduce me to her dog, Molly, who gave me a big toothy grin when I greeted her. The whole interaction left me with a rather melancholy feeling in my gut, though I couldn't pinpoint why. And yet, a smile pulls at the corners of my mouth as I think about it now.

I park at the train station—dizzy, but calm. My head hurts like a son of a bitch, but I don't think it's bad enough to warrant a trip to the hospital.

From here, it's another hour and a half to work. My long commute allows me far too much time to sit and ponder all that's wrong with my life. I board the train, a bit unsteadily, and settle into a window seat. I close my eyes and replay the argument from this morning in my head. Kate's angry, overwhelmed face swims around through the darkness.

What happened to us? Is this just a phase? Or the natural progression of things? I'm not sure I can live like this forever. It's certainly not what I had in mind when I said "I do." I still love Kate, but love isn't enough anymore.

I pull out my phone and glance at it every few minutes, hoping for an apology text. But what does she have to apologize for? She's right. Most of this is my fault. I'm the one screwing up. Not trying hard enough, not seeing her side of things. Why am I so resistant to talking about the hard stuff? Probably because I know it'll start a fight. But perhaps it wouldn't if I didn't avoid it for so long.

I'm lightheaded, and my eyelids are getting heavy. People walking down the aisle of the train shoot concerned glances at me as they pass. My head continues to ache, the pain blooming out in every direction.

A woman catches my eye as she walks toward me down the aisle. She's glancing around for a place to sit, and her movements give off an air of carefree energy. Maybe she'll sit next to me. She pauses briefly to observe the empty seat beside me, flashes a polite smile, and continues down the train. Oh well.

I'm fighting to stay awake, despite the fact that I could use a little rest after the morning I've had. But if I fall asleep on the train I might miss my stop, and I can't afford that.

An hour later I arrive at work and continue my mundane, daily routine: check my email, check my phone for an apology text or voicemail, go to a meeting, go to lunch, accomplish afternoon tasks, accept unfamiliar high-dosage painkillers from a co-worker I barely know, check my phone again for apology, check email for apology, recognize that my head feels fuzzy and regret taking unfamiliar high-dosage painkillers from a co-worker I barely know, tell my boss I'm fine when he asks if I'm okay, take a minute to study the framed picture of Kate on my desk, and realize the minute has turned into the rest of my workday. I leave, ready to repeat my long commute with the sun shining on the other side of the tracks.

I step aboard the train around 5:00 p.m. The day has been a blur. I walk down the aisle, searching again for a spot with two empty seats so I can sit next to a window. I find one and then proceed to watch the currents of people swirling around the train, looking for their proper places. We all do it. It's such an insignificant event in the grand scheme of things, but at that particular moment, it's everything.

What type of person will sit next to me today? A friendly woman? Not likely. An old man? More likely. Someone loud who talks on the phone the entire ride or plays music through their headphones at an intrusive volume? Even more likely.

Random thoughts flit through my mind as I drift off to sleep. Will Kate be just as mad when I get home? Will it still be tense and awkward? Of course it will. She probably wants nothing to do with me. She probably has her bags packed. Or mine. Did I pay the water bill yet? Shit, what else did I forget? This last thought causes my brain to work a little harder than it wants to, which stalls my sleep for a few extra seconds, but ultimately loses the battle.

I stumble into a strange, chaotic dream. I'm stuck in some third world country, trying to protect my kids from terrorists. We're hiding in a small, cluttered house. A man dressed in black enters the room, holding a machine gun. We crouch down behind a counter. My daughters are scared, so I cover them with my body and close my eyes, praying he doesn't find us. I sense him approaching and hold my breath. He presses the barrel of the gun against my head. The trigger squeaks as he tenses his finger. This is it; I'm going to die. The last thought I have is, *Poor Kate. She's going to be so devastated when she finds out.* He pulls the trigger. I wait for the pain to strike, but it never arrives.

CHAPTER SIX

STRANGER DANGER?

I jerk awake and look wildly about me, unsure of where I am. There's a woman sitting in the seat next to me with long caramel-colored hair, her eyes wide with surprise. She's holding her hands up like she's under arrest.

"Are you okay?" she asks with a chuckle.

I sit up, embarrassed, glancing around as I try to get my bearings. "Yeah... I think so." I look at her. "I was dreaming."

She lowers her hands to her lap. "Must have been some dream. You nearly gave me a black eye."

"Sorry about that. I'll try to keep myself under control."

"No worries." She crosses one leg over the other. She's dressed in business attire: high heels, navy blue skirt, and a white blouse that shows off just enough cleavage to be sexy but not inappropriate. "Did you make it out alive?" she asks.

"Excuse me?"

"In your dream. Did you survive?"

"No... I don't think I did."

She reaches up and pushes her hair back behind her shoulder. "Bummer." She stares straight ahead, swinging her foot back and forth to a rhythm that I can't hear.

My headache is gone. There's no pain at all. I rub my eyes and look out the window, realizing I have no idea where I am. "Do you know which stop is next?" I ask her.

She peers out the window beside me, perplexed. "Belmont, I think." She leans in to get a closer look, bringing her face within a few inches of mine. Her closeness suggests we're friends instead of strangers. I can't help but gaze at the side of her face as she studies the view outside. She's radiant, with perfect olive-colored skin, hazel eyes, and shiny hair that looks as soft and smooth as silk. Her perfume smells amazing as well— a field of wildflowers that envelops me and drowns out all the unpleasant memories from this morning. As if sensing my gaze, she looks at me, her eyes settling directly into mine, then she settles back into her chair, flushed. She clears her throat. "Yes, Belmont is next. I'm sure of it."

Her lips continue moving, but I don't hear the words. I'm spellbound. Everything goes blurry, and I blink several times before my vision clears.

"I'm sorry?" I say.

Her smile broadens. "I asked if that's your stop."

"Oh, yes. It is. Thanks. I'm glad I didn't miss it. What about you?"

A quizzical brow arches above her left eye. "Am I glad you didn't miss it?"

I laugh, surprising myself with the sound—I haven't laughed for days. "No, I mean, which stop is yours?"

"Oh." She chuckles. "Same one, actually."

"Really?"

"Mm-hmm. I'm glad you said something. I almost missed it, myself."

"Do you take this train regularly?" I ask.

She nods. "I do."

"I'm surprised I've never seen you before. I've been taking this train for years."

"I guess our paths just never crossed. Our timing must have been off."

"Yeah…" I say. "Must have been."

I stare out the window, waiting to arrive at our destination. The urge to continue talking to her fills my chest. It's refreshing to chat with someone new. There's no rut to get stuck in, no preconceived notions to struggle against. She won't fault me for saying the wrong thing.

I turn toward her and open my mouth, preparing to speak again, but the sight of her steals any half-formed sentences from my mind. My eyes are caught on her smooth, tanned legs. The hem of her skirt cuts a sleek line across her thighs, and she isn't wearing any stockings. I try to look away, but her legs fill my vision, encompassing every inch of space between her and me. A pleasant but inconvenient road block. She crosses one leg over the other, and I force my eyes back up to her face.

"So, what kind of work do you do?" I ask.

She takes a quick, calculated breath before answering. "I work in the medical field."

"Wow. That's great," I say. This morning's conversation with Kate about her mysterious medical appointment springs to mind. "Any specific medical field?"

She tilts her head back and forth like she's weighing her answer. "More in the scientific realm. I'm assisting in the creation and development of various types of medication." She shrugs. "That's all I can really say about it." She flashes an apologetic frown. "Sorry."

"No problem. I understand. Sounds cool, though. You work in the city, I assume?"

"I do, yes. How about you? What do you do?"

"Computer stuff."

"Ah… Any specific computer stuff?" She smirks.

I smirk back. "It varies. I'm currently working on a multi-year system transition project…integrated with thirty-plus other vendors and at least that many systems."

"So basically, you're a computer geek?"

I shrug. "I guess you could say that."

She shifts in her seat. "No offense."

An automated voice announces over the speaker that our stop is approaching, and the train slows.

"Guess this is us," I say.

"Guess so."

"Well, it was nice chatting with you." I hold my hand out. "I'm Ron, by the way."

"Hi, Ron." She shakes my hand. Her hand feels surprisingly warm and moist, like mine is when I'm nervous. "Courtney. Nice chatting with you, too."

Her smile lingers, as does our handshake, causing my insides to do a few strange, wonderful flips. The kind you feel when you first meet and connect with someone you're attracted to. I had forgotten what it felt like, and I never imagined I would feel it again.

The train comes to a stop. We stand and walk out together. Once we're outside, the crowd separates us, but we end up side by side once again at the crosswalk in front of the parking garage. At first, she doesn't realize that we've been pushed back together. I take the opportunity to study her out of the corner of my eye. She's wearing diamond earrings that sparkle like stars. She's also wearing an expensive-looking gold bracelet around her wrist. Kate only wears jewelry on special occasions.

She turns her head and notices me. "Oh, hey."

"Hello again," I say.

"Long time no see." The wind blows her hair around. She tucks it back behind her ears and smiles.

We wait for the light to change.

I glance up at the sunset tinged white, fluffy clouds in the sky. "Beautiful evening, huh?"

"Gorgeous," she says. "It finally feels like spring." The breeze returns and tosses her hair around again. The playful gusts of wind grab ahold of her perfume and carry it along. My head spins as it curls around me.

"Sure does…"

She runs her hands through her hair a couple of times, straightening it out, then holds it in place behind her head like a ponytail and lets it go. "Let's hope it stays this way."

The sign signals us to proceed.

We get to the garage, and I hold the door open for her. She thanks me and leads the way up the stairs. My eyes stay glued to her finely-toned calves with each step. I'm nervous but don't know why. When we reach the second level, she heads toward the door as a stream of people flows between us, working its way around me.

"I'll see you later!" I yell.

She looks back at me and says, "Take care, Ron," then disappears through the door.

I make my way up to the third floor, feeling like a kid whose birthday cake was just stolen out from under him, just as he was blowing out the candles.

Walking to my car, every detail of this woman is etched into my brain: her scent, her eyes, her calm, soothing voice... I can't shake it. Courtney. Excitement bubbles inside me, and I can't stop smiling. Positive energy runs rampant inside of me. I could run a marathon right now.

This isn't good. How did this happen?

I get to my car and try to open the door, but it doesn't move. My new dent stares back at me as if to say, "What did you expect?" I push one foot up against the car and pull the handle as hard as I can until it finally pops open, screeching like the gates of hell. I get in, roll the windows down for some air, and rest my head against the steering wheel.

"What's wrong with me?" I ask myself out loud. "Calm down, Ron. She's only a woman. Yes, she's pretty. Yes, she's friendly. Big deal. There's no reason to obsess over it. Move on and get home to your wife."

I look to my left and see a man in the driver's seat of the car next to me, staring at me. Listening. Next time I argue with myself, I might want to check to see if I'm alone first.

"Hi there," I say, starting the car. "I was just leaving—" Music blasts, assaulting my ears again. I punch the power button with my fist. The man continues staring. "Sorry," I mutter. I reverse out of the parking spot and drive away.

I drive slowly down the spiral pathways of the garage.

I wish I'd had more time to talk to her. To learn more about her. She was so refreshing. So calm and attentive. Quick to smile. I can't help imagining how smoothly this morning would have gone if I were married to someone like her. I can never break through to Kate. She wants us to spend time together, but when we *are* together, she pushes me away, and we both end up feeling alone because the walls she builds are impenetrable.

Whenever I try to get close to her, she rejects me. We can never have a natural conversation like the one I had with Courtney—when we talk, I just end up exhausted.

Maybe I'll run into Courtney tomorrow. The thought of it sparks excitement in my gut.

There's nothing wrong with talking to her. It's not like I'll do anything inappropriate. I'm married. I've never even thought about cheating on Kate, at least not seriously. I don't know why I'm even contemplating this. Chances are I'll never see Courtney again. She's no different from the crowds of people I pass by on a daily basis. There one moment, gone forever the next. A phantom face in a sea of equally unreal faces. The only difference was a short conversation.

And then I see her again. Up ahead, leaning forward underneath the hood of her bright yellow VW Beetle convertible. What are the odds? I pull up behind her and clear my throat, making my presence known.

She jumps a little in surprise, almost banging her head as she straightens from examining her engine. "Oh, hey. You again."

"Me again. Car trouble?"

"It appears that way. I can't get the damn thing to start. I must look like a fool, huh?" She wrinkles her nose in annoyance.

"Not at all. Anything I can do to help?"

"I sure hope so. Are you any good with cars?" She shoots a glance at the dent in my door.

I shrug. "I know a few things. Hold on; let me park." I pull into a nearby spot. I know precisely nothing about cars. But what else am I going to do? Apologize and drive away?

I pull the handle and push the door to get out, but it won't open. I push as hard as I can. Still nothing. I exit through the passenger side, grateful for the two cars blocking her view of my struggles, and walk over to her.

"All right, let's take a look," I say. I fiddle around with a few wires under the hood, trying to appear like I have a clue, while hoping to discover an obvious solution like a giant tube hanging down that just needs to be reconnected. But of course, that doesn't happen.

After what seems like a sufficient amount of time, I stand up straight and rub my hands together like a mechanic. "It doesn't look good, I'm afraid."

"It doesn't?"

I shake my head. "Nope. I hate to say it, but you might need to have it towed."

She crosses her arms and frowns. "Well, that's wonderful."

"Sorry."

"It's not your fault."

I close the hood. "I know a decent place that won't screw you."

"Well, that's always a plus," she says. "Any help at all would be great, thanks. I'm a bit of a mess today."

"It's no problem." I wait, expecting her to pull out her phone so I can give her the number, but instead she continues standing there like she's not sure what to do. "Do you need to use my phone?"

"If you don't mind. I forgot mine at home this morning."

"Sure, no problem." I take my phone out of my pocket, scroll to the number of the towing company, and hold it out for her to take.

She hesitates. "That's not all," she says.

I drop my hand back down to my side. "Okay…?"

"I also forgot my wallet."

"Dang, you *are* a mess."

"I told you." She swats me on the arm playfully, and I try to ignore the way my skin tingles in the wake of her touch. "Don't pick on me."

I laugh.

"I'm not usually such an airhead. It's been one of those days."

"Hasn't it, though? My day hasn't been too swell either."

"Hmm," she says, thoughtfully. "Must be something in the stars." She smiles.

I smile back. "So what now?"

"Well, unless you're going to pay for the tow, which I can't ask you to do, the only option I see is for me to leave my car here tonight. I'll come back for it in the morning after I get my phone and wallet."

"Makes sense. I could drive you home, then pick you up in the morning and drop you off here. It's on my way, obviously."

"Thanks, Ron. That's sweet of you to offer. Only… You can't take me home."

"I can't?"

She shakes her head, grinning like she has a secret.

"And why is that?" I ask.

She puts her hands on her hips. "Because, technically, I don't have a home to go to at the moment."

I blink in surprise. "Wow, this just keeps getting more and more interesting."

"Don't I know it."

"So you're homeless?"

"Not exactly." She leans against the hood of her car and heaves a sigh. I stand next to her and do the same, close enough that our shoulders brush against each other. "I'm between apartments right now. My lease ran out on my old place, but I'm moving to my new apartment in about a week. In the meantime, I'm staying with a friend of mine. Most of my stuff is in storage. It's been a big pain in the ass, honestly."

"Gotcha. So I should probably take you to your friend's house then, right?"

She hesitates. "Yeah, that would make the most sense."

We both laugh.

"I'm sorry I'm so out of it," she says. "Clearly, I'm not thinking straight."

"It's okay; it happens to me all the time."

She giggles. "I'm not on drugs; I swear."

"Sure you're not," I say, nudging her arm with my elbow. I glance past my shoulder into her car and notice an oversized coat on the passenger's seat.

"It used to be my dad's," she says. "He hates to see me in thin jackets, so whenever I visit him, I throw that on."

I nod. My gut tells me there's a missing piece to that puzzle, but I'm not in the right mindset to put it together.

"I'll lock my car and meet you at yours," she says.

"Sounds good." I bolt to my car, excited. I pull on the door handle, forgetting that it's stuck in place. Once again, it doesn't move. I don't want to make a scene, so I go around through the passenger side again and climb across. I glance up at the dents on the padded ceiling and run my fingers across them. They appear fainter than they had this morning, as if they'd healed throughout the day.

My head is spinning. I can't help noticing the many ways in which Courtney differs from Kate. Not just personality-wise, but physically too. She's shorter by an inch or so. Thinner. More delicate. Her hair is straighter, and her skin is tan. All of these differences, on top of how quiet and laid-back she is, leave no doubt in my mind that she's one hundred percent Kate's opposite. I'm not sure if that's a good or a bad thing yet.

I grab Kate's coat and toss it into the back seat just before Courtney opens the door and gets in.

She glances around as she pulls the seat belt over her chest. "Cool car."

"Thanks." I assume she's being sarcastic and anticipate a peach joke.

"No, I mean it. It's very...retro. I love the paint job."

I do my best to remain calm while doing a happy dance in my head. This chick is awesome. "Seriously? You like it?"

"Yeah, what's not to like?"

"Well, I know it's not the most attractive car in the world, but it runs well. Never has any mechanical problems..." I glance at her.

Her smile fades.

"Sorry. I didn't mean it like that."

"It's fine; I get it," she says, her voice edgy and cold.

My heart races. "I wasn't talking about *your* car..."

She nods, but the hurt on her face is still evident.

"All right, I was. But it was just a joke. I'm sorry if I—"

She bursts into laughter, grabbing onto my arm with a firm grip. "Calm down, Ron! I'm totally messing with you."

I chuckle with relief. "You had me going there for a second."

"I sure did." Our combined laughter comes to an end as she looks up at the ceiling, observing my knuckle dents. "Did you have an accident?"

"Why do you ask?"

"Well, I noticed the dent on your door when you pulled up, and your ceiling looks a little rough. So, I thought maybe you had an accident." Her tone is so sweet and full of concern that suddenly I'm fighting the urge to get closer to her. Possibly even kiss her. "So did you?" she asks.

"Something like that."

She raises her eyebrows.

"Come on," I say. "Let's get out of here."

I start the engine, and the music hits my ears like a tsunami. We both flinch back against our seats, and I fumble to switch it off.

She clears her throat. "Feeling a bit angsty, are we?"

"Are you okay?" I ask, slightly out of breath.

She makes a face like she's trying not to smile. "Yes, I'm fine. A bit deaf, perhaps, but I think I'll live."

"Sorry, I should have warned you. My stereo has a mind of its own." I shift gears and pull out of the parking space, making it out of the garage without further incident.

"So where we headed?" I ask.

"Route 86, please. Just stay on that for three or four miles, then take exit three."

"Got it."

"Is that too far?" she asks.

"Nope."

Neither of us says anything for a couple of minutes, which is just as well, since I can't think of anything interesting to say next. So much for being good at small talk. No wonder Kate is bored with me. Which reminds me...

I grab my cell phone. "Excuse me a sec; I need to make a quick call."

"No problem," she says.

I dial Kate's number, already nervous and unsure of what to expect. She picks up on the second ring. "Hello?" Her voice is deadpan, as usual.

"Hi," I say.

Silence.

"Hello?" I ask.

"Yeah?"

"Hey, it's me."

"Obviously," she says. "What's up? Something wrong?"

"No, why?"

"Because you never call me on your way home unless something is wrong."

"Oh." I make a mental note to call more often.

"So, what's up?" she asks.

"Nothing. Everything's fine. I just wanted to tell you that I'm giving someone a ride home. Their car wouldn't start. So, I'll be a little late."

"How late?"

"Not sure. Fifteen, twenty minutes."

"Okay, but don't take too long. Dinner's almost ready."

"All right, I won't. I'll see you soon."

"All right... So who's your guest?"

"My guest?" I ask.

"Yeah, the other person in the car with you. What are they like? Man? Woman? Old? Young?"

"Um..."

"There better not be some gorgeous woman there with you."

"There's not," I say.

Not necessarily a lie. Beauty is in the eye of the beholder, after all.

"So, it's a man then?" she asks.

"What's that?"

"It's a man? In the car with you?"

I glance at Courtney. She glances back at me, her eyes radiating curiosity. "Yes."

Okay, just a small white lie. No need to rock the boat more by adding jealousy into the mix.

"Why didn't you just say that before?"

"I don't know. You know my brain runs slow after work."

She snorts. "That's an understatement."

"All right, well..."

"Okay, come home. I miss you!"

The tension leaves my body in a rush. "All of a sudden?"

"Yeah... Maybe... I'm sorry I was such a bitch this morning."

"It's okay."

"No, I mean it. I took time today to think about everything that's been going on between us. I've been taking my frustrations out on you too much, and I'm sorry. It's not fair to you. I miss you. I don't want to argue anymore."

A reassuring warmth enters my chest. "Me too."

"And I'll try to be more pleasant in the mornings."

"What about the evenings?"

"Don't push it."

I laugh. Her teasing tone has put me at ease.

"The house is nice and quiet. I have a romantic dinner planned for us."

"*Do* you?"

"Mm-hmm."

"Sounds great," I say. Why is she being so sweet? Now I feel twice as guilty.

"Did you call the phone company today and ask them about the extra fee?"

"No, I forgot."

"Of course you did."

And the guilt leaves again, right out the window.

"Will you do that, please?" she continues. "Like right now, even. I bet they're still open."

"I'll do it tomorrow," I say.

"Okay, but don't forget."

"I won't."

"Promise?"

"I promise."

"You've promised before."

I stop talking and let the silence breathe between us for a moment, hoping that she's finally ready to hang up.

"How was work today?" she asks.

"Kate."

"Yeah?"

"I'll be home in a few minutes. We don't need to hash out our entire day, right now over the phone, while I'm driving. Plus, I have company, so I'm being rude."

"All right, fine. I love you, bye."

"Love you too." I hang up and stick the phone in my jacket pocket, exasperated. Courtney and I exchange awkward glances.

"Sooo, how long have you been married?" Courtney asks.

"Who? Me? I'm not married. That was my roommate, Bob."

"Oh, Bob. Of course. And I suppose Kate is...what? His nickname?"

"Yes, yes it is."

"Strange nickname."

"Isn't it? I keep telling him he should change it to something else, like Robert, but he never listens."

She giggles. "Funny."

"Not really. It's pretty complicated, actually."

"What is? Bob?"

"Yes, Bob."

"You love Bob," she says, with a hushed seriousness.

"I do."

"So, you're gay?"

"Yup."

"Interesting. I wouldn't have guessed that about you."

"No? How come? I don't fit the stereotype?"

"Well, there is that, yes. But, I was referring more to the way you keep looking at my legs. And how you blush a little whenever we make eye contact."

I chuckle nervously. "I have no idea what you're talking about." Heat washes through my face. "I'm blushing right now, aren't I?"

She nods. "Yup."

"Darn," I say. Then, after a pause: "Twelve years."

"Impressive. You look so young. How old are you anyway?"

"Twenty-two."

"Wow. It must have been quite something, getting married when you were ten."

"Yeah, it wasn't too bad, actually. We went to the playground for our honeymoon. I pushed her on the swings."

She laughs.

"I'm thirty-three," I say.

"Now that sounds more realistic. It must be hard, staying faithful to one woman your whole life. Especially when you get married so young."

"Some days are harder than others," I say.

"I bet. Is she pretty?"

"Yep."

"Funny?"

"Oh, yes."

"Caring?"

"Um...she can be. On her good days. Is the interview over yet?"

"Sorry, I was just curious." She leans back in her seat and gets more comfortable. "Any kids?"

"Three."

"Wow, that's great. Boys or girls?"

"Three beautiful, brown-eyed, brown-haired little girls."

"Aww, so cute," she says. "How old are they? What are their names?"

"Well, there's Evelyn, my oldest and wisest," I begin.

"I love that name," she says, smiling broadly. "Gorgeous."

"She's eleven and tough as nails. Smart too, and boy does she know it. Then there's Lilly, my eight-year-old. She's got more emotions than she knows what to do with—more than *we* know what to do with half the time. She takes life very seriously."

"Cute."

"She's my little drama queen. She never hesitates to cry when she's overwhelmed and never does anything without a good amount of forethought."

"She sounds sweet."

"She is. And finally, there's Olivia, who's three and quite sassy. She keeps us all in line, as well as entertained. She never fails to make me laugh."

"They all sound amazing, Ron. I'd love to meet them someday."

I nod, unsure of how to respond. "Yeah...maybe." A brief scenario plays out in my head where I see Courtney sitting on the floor with them, laughing as they all play a game together. She looks up at me with seductive eyes as I enter the room, and I smile back, pleased with how well they're getting along...

"I can tell how much you love those girls," she says. "Your soul shines when you talk about them."

"It does?"

"Mm-hmm. Not so much when you speak about your wife though, I'm afraid."

I nod, pressing my lips together tightly. "How about you?" I ask, desperate to change the subject. "Any kids?"

"Me? No, no. Not yet. No room in my life right now. I'm going to wait until I'm a little older and not so focused on my career. I finally finished medical school this past year, and it feels like I'm always busy. Thankfully, though, all my hard work seems to be paying off."

"Wonderful," I say, only half-listening. My mind is still drifting. I try to imagine what a child of hers would look like. I envision an adorable, light-haired little girl, smiling. If things were different and I had a daughter with Courtney, what would she look like? What would it be like? How different would it be from raising kids with Kate?

"Don't get me wrong," she says. "I love kids. I really do. I'd love to have a couple of my own someday, if I can find the right man for the job before I'm ninety."

"Nonsense. You don't need a man to have kids."

She laughs, sounding genuinely amused. "That's true, I suppose. But having a father in the picture would be nice. Preferably a kind, loving, gentle one...like you."

Without even looking, I can feel her eyes burning through me. "Well, I have no doubt that you'll find someone who makes you happy and have a couple beautiful babies of your own someday."

"One can only hope." She smirks. "Thank you, though."

We sit in silence for a couple of minutes.

"Are we getting close?" I ask, trying to distract myself from whatever is welling up inside of me.

"Yeah, kind of. We still have a few more miles to go. Just keep going straight down this road. I'll tell you when to stop."

"Got it." The realization that we'll be parting soon arrives with a sense of sadness, like it did in the parking garage. Not much time left to talk. "So, how come you didn't stay in your previous apartment?"

"Well, like I said, my lease was up."

"Right, but couldn't you have renewed it?"

"Yeah, but I didn't want to. It was too big for me, not to mention expensive. And since it's only me, alone and single, I figured it'd be more logical for me to move into something smaller and more affordable."

I rub my chin thoughtfully. "Makes sense."

Why did she feel the need to mention that she's both "alone" and "single?" Is she trying to give me a hint? Is she emphasizing how available she is?

"Why did you rent such a big apartment in the first place?" I ask.

"I moved in with someone else, initially. But he moved out about six months ago."

"Sorry to hear that."

"Don't be. It was for the best. I don't mind being single. It certainly has its perks. But it can get lonely sometimes too. You know?"

I nod. I think about telling her how being married can feel just as lonely, if not worse. But I catch myself at the last second and tuck it away to the back of my mouth, where the rest of the words best left unsaid reside.

I picture her inside her previous apartment, alone every night in her oversized bed, wishing someone was there to hold her and keep her safe.

"You start to miss certain…things when you're single," she continues. "You know, things you married people don't have to worry about."

"If you're saying what I think you're saying, then trust me, I still have to worry. Just this morning, in fact—" I cut myself off. Why am I revealing such personal information to someone I just met?

She scoffs, "Whatever."

"I'm serious. Everything you've heard is a myth. One of those urban legends single people are taught early on, but it's not true. Marriage is far from perfect. There's still plenty of loneliness, despair, sexual frustration, masturbation."

"Oh my," she says, raising an eyebrow.

"Sorry. Didn't mean to get carried away."

"No, please. Keep going. This is fascinating."

"Hardly," I say. "More like depressing. Let's change the subject."

"Whatever you say. You say it's a myth, but I promise it won't be that way for me when I'm married. I plan on spoiling my husband with love and affection every chance I get."

I snort. "You say that now... Until he forgets to take the laundry out of the washer, and suddenly you're cursing his name every time you catch a whiff of that sour smell."

"Trust me, that wouldn't be enough to make me angry. I'm pretty easy going in case you didn't notice. Plus, my husband won't be handling the laundry, anyway."

"Well, your future husband is a lucky guy then."

"And with Kate only working part-time, she should already have that stuff finished when you get home, in my opinion."

"Well, she's busy doing other things..." I scratch my head. "How'd you know Kate only works part-time?"

Courtney's eyes widen. "What do you mean?"

"I don't recall mentioning it earlier."

She shrugs. "I don't know. You must have brought it up at some point."

"Yeah, I guess... Anyway, she gets it done most of the time. I'm not complaining about that. She does way more than I could ever handle. I was thinking more of like, weekends and stuff."

Courtney blinks a few times.

"Never mind," I say. "It's a lot harder than you think. That's all I'm saying."

"Well, regardless, I still believe that if you're patient, and wait long enough to find someone who's truly perfect for you... Then the myth becomes reality."

"That's a very nice fairy tale to believe in."

One side of her mouth curls up into a sarcastic smile, but she keeps listening as I go on.

"People being perfect for each other is a myth in itself," I say. "You just need to find a 'good enough' person to share your life with and make it worthwhile."

"Good enough person?"

"Yeah. That and follow the recipe for marital satisfaction, and you'll be a lot less likely to hate your life."

"Recipe for marital satisfaction, huh?"

"That's right," I say.

"And you got this from where?"

I point to my head.

"Is that so?"

"Mm-hmm."

"All right, Mr. Know-It-All…" She removes her seat belt and repositions her body, tucking her legs underneath her and resting her elbows on the center console. She cups her chin in the palm of her hand and focuses on me with curious eyes, ready and willing to give me her undivided attention. "Please, tell me your recipe for marital satisfaction. I must hear it."

"You really want to know?"

She nods several times. "Very much."

"All right then." I clear my throat, feeling oddly like one of my old high school teachers preparing for a lecture. "First, you need to find someone with whom you have chemistry. Some-one you can tolerate enough to survive living together for the rest of your life, while always maintaining a mutual respect for one another." I hold my right index finger in the air. "Respect. Very important. If you don't respect each other, it'll never work."

"Respect," she repeats. "Got it."

"Also, in order for your marriage to succeed, you must fulfill a few initial requirements, such as ensuring that you share at least a couple of common interests and goals. Next…"

My eyes slide off of the road for a moment and connect with hers. She smiles encouragingly, and I keep going.

"Assume that your spouse will probably drive you nuts at least half the time, if not most, but just love him to death regardless. And last but not least, you must accept all of his idiosyncrasies, issues, bizarre hobbies, strange habits, faults, emotional baggage, and harmless mistakes as if they're your own. And that's it."

"Wow," she says.

"Yup. I'm telling you, if people followed those rules, they'd be good to go."

"Impressive."

I shrug.

"You've put a lot of thought into this."

"Sure have."

"And how many of these rules have you and your wife followed?"

I'm hesitant to answer. "Not enough…"

"And what if you were single right now?"

I glance at her.

"Would you say that you and I are off to a decent start on your little checklist?"

She runs her finger down the side of my arm and then holds it in place. Soon, the rest of her fingers join in. Her touch is light—practically non-existent—yet the weight of her words add to it substantially.

"Yeah, maybe. Hard to tell… We just met." The words fall stuttering from my mouth as I try to think.

What would it be like if I were married to Courtney? Would I be happier? Would I feel more rested in the morning? I'm sure she has a few skeletons in her closet, like everyone else. Or some less-than-wonderful personality traits that I haven't picked up on in the first hour that I've known her. She might be a slob or a terrible mother. It's hard to imagine anyone being a better mother than Kate. But, if things don't work out between Kate and me, if the rift between us has grown too large, it's not too late to start over. I can picture myself dating Courtney. Taking it slow at first and then eventually falling in love. We already get along well. I never did get a chance to date much, because Kate and I married so young. I would even be willing to have another baby. Kate's tubes are tied, so no more options there. It would be like a second phase of life. There's nothing wrong with that. People do it all the time. It wouldn't take anything away from what we've already accomplished.

But what about the life that Kate and I built together? Year after year, brick by emotional brick. Could I allow it all to be bulldozed to the ground? We haven't accomplished all we set out to do yet. And what about the girls? They'd be devastated. Wouldn't they? Kids are resilient, though. They'd still see us both. Just…separately. Which is more or less how it is already.

"Ron?"

"Hmm?"

"You okay?"

"Yeah, why?"

"You got kind of quiet on me."

"Sorry, I'm just feeling a bit spacey. My mind wanders when I get tired."

"What, am I boring you?" she smirks. Her hand is still resting on my arm.

"Not at all. It's just been a long day." I yawn.

Courtney yawns as well, and leans her head back against the seat. She slides her heels off with her toes and stretches her legs out, resting her bare feet on the dashboard.

"Make yourself at home," I say.

"Thanks, I will." She shifts her body toward me again. "So, Ron, what do you do in your spare time when you're not rescuing young women from despair inside parking garages?"

I snort. "Shouldn't we be there by now?" I ask.

"Yeah, not too much farther."

It feels like I'm driving cross country. Where the hell does her friend live?

Courtney raises her eyebrows. "Well?"

"What? You really want to know about my spare time?"

"Of course."

"Well, let's see. I play with my kids, watch movies, work on home projects...I don't know. Spare time? What's that?"

"Raising a family must be difficult."

"It can be. Sometimes, the hardest part is just trying to please multiple people at once."

"I can imagine."

"I do have one hobby."

"What's that?"

I smirk. "Building treehouses."

Her eyes light up. "For real?" She sits up straight.

"Yup."

"I love treehouses."

"Really?"

"Yes, really. I even watch that show where they build those crazy big ones. I'd so live in a treehouse."

"Every summer, we go into our back woods and either add onto a previous treehouse or start a new one. Sometimes we finish it, sometimes we don't. My daughters always help. They love handing me the tools and have a blast playing inside them when we're finished."

"That is *so* cool! I would have killed to have my father do something like that with me when I was young. Your family is lucky to have you."

"Thanks." An assuring warmth spreads through my chest.

"I hope when I'm married someday that my husband has fun with my kids like that."

"We do have a lot of fun together. It gets on Kate's nerves sometimes, though. She says I play *too* much. That I act like a kid myself half the time."

"Hey, better than spending no time with them at all. You could be an abusive prick."

"Exactly! That's what I always say."

"You sound like an amazing father to me, Ron."

"You think so?"

"I really do. I've known a lot of men, and most of the time they're never as decent, or as genuine, as you appear to be."

"Thanks, Courtney. I appreciate that. So…no boyfriend, huh?"

"Nope."

"How come?"

She shrugs her shoulders. "The guys I date are never worth getting serious about. They're either too immature or self-centered or controlling. Sometimes all three at once. It's frustrating."

"I'm sure it is," I say.

"It is. You don't know." She shoves my shoulder. "Jerk."

"What? I was being serious!" I chuckle.

"Sure you were."

I reach up past my bangs and scratch near the wound.

Her eyes widen with concern. "Oh my goodness, what happened to your head?" She leans in close, placing her hand on my leg for support as she moves my hair aside to examine the wound. Her intoxicating smell and warm breath bouncing off my cheek are almost enough to make me drive off the road. I do my best to maintain my composure and drive a straight line. "What happened?" she repeats.

"It's nothing. I was in a minor car accident this morning. My car slid off the road. That's how I got the dent on the door. I'm fine, though, honest."

"You poor thing... It doesn't look fine. It looks like it hurts. It's all swollen..." She massages her fingers against the back of my head in small circles. "You might need stitches." I hit a bump in the road, causing her body to jolt closer to me. She doesn't seem to mind. She's so close, her chest is pressed against my arm. I'm staring at the road, but again, I can feel her eyes burning a hole through me. I glance at her. "We should go to the hospital," she says.

I snicker. "Don't be ridiculous."

She moves back away from me a bit so that our bodies are no longer touching. "Come on, what are you afraid of? It'll be fun. I'll even hold your hand while they stitch you up. I'm pretty good at taking care of people, you know?"

"I bet you are." We exchange playful glances. "I'll be fine. Thanks, though."

"Suit yourself."

A brief moment of silence condenses in the air, allowing us to collect our thoughts, and possibly re-evaluate our intentions.

"Ron?"

"Yeah?" I ask, suddenly beaming with anticipation.

"You're about to pass my street."

I stomp my foot against the brakes and cut the wheel to the left. My tires screech and emit the awful scent of burnt rubber as I swing a hard left onto Cleveland Avenue, driving over the curb and then coming to an immediate stop. She topples forward onto me, grabbing my shoulder with one hand and planting her palm against the roof with the other.

At this moment, my lips are touching her neck, and her hair is draped over my face. "Sorry about that," I say.

She leans back enough to stare into my eyes, her hand still gripped on my shoulder, her mouth a few inches from mine. My eyes meet her gaze as she moves her raised hand down to my head and brushes my bangs over to one side. "Close one. Good thing you didn't hurt your head again."

"Yeah… Good thing." During this brief moment, when the loneliness that appears to dwell inside us both crawls out, naked and vulnerable, to embrace in the open, I'm sure that she's going to kiss me.

But she doesn't. Instead, she takes her hands off of me and leans back against her seat, quiet and serious.

"Now where?" I ask.

She stares ahead, scanning the street. "Fourth house on the left."

I drive forward. "The…brown one?" I can't quite make out what the hell color it is.

"That's the one."

As we approach the house, I struggle to balance the mixed emotions rumbling inside of me. I'm disappointed she's leaving because I'm really enjoying her company. But that's why I need her to leave. I don't want to do anything I'm going to regret.

I forgot how much I missed the amazing feeling of meeting someone new. It's so rare to reside in that discovery of instant chemistry between two strangers and wonder where it will lead. Everything is still mysterious and exciting, charging the air with energy. Sure, there are ways to spice up a marriage, but it's not the same. Nothing can match that initial spark that pulls and tears at both your gut and your heart with equal measure.

I pull into the fourth driveway on the left and observe the sad looking house in front of us. I'm not sure what I imagined when I pictured the house in my head, but it sure as hell wasn't this. It's a small, decrepit old home that doesn't look anything like the other houses on this street. The hair on the back of my neck stands up as I lean forward to get a better view. Vines obscure the entire front side of the house, and the lawn is overgrown. It's dark too. Not a single light on inside. Is this really where her friend lives? I almost feel bad, dropping her off here.

"I appreciate the ride, Ron. You're a lifesaver."

"Sure thing. Glad I could help. I enjoyed chatting with you."

"Yeah, me too," she says. "I owe you one. Thanks for teaching me the secrets of life." She winks. Then, she places her hand on my left cheek and leans in to kiss the other. My head swims. She smiles sweetly, massaging my fingers with hers. She hesitates like she might say more, then exits the car. And just like that... She's gone. Back to reality. It's kind of a relief, actually.

I shake my head as I watch her saunter toward the front door. "Un-be-lievable," I mumble under my breath.

Now that there's some distance between us, and this is probably the last time I'll see her, I already feel ridiculous and guilty for entertaining the thought of kissing her and betraying Kate. Thank God I didn't. Time to get my head back out of the clouds.

But wait. Didn't I already agree to pick her up in the morning and take her back to her car? I can't remember. Maybe I didn't. If I did, she never brought it up again, so maybe she forgot. I could yell to her now and double check.

I place my finger on the button to lower the window but hesitate. If I bring it up now she's likely to take me up on it. Then I'm guaranteed to see her again, which would only lead to more temptation.

I put both of my hands firmly back on the wheel. She'll be fine. She's not my responsibility, after all. She can always call a taxi or another friend to help her. No, it's definitely best that I leave now, while I have the chance.

CHAPTER SEVEN

THE ARRANGEMENT

I shift into reverse with a sense of satisfaction, eager to get home and see Kate. I begin backing out of the driveway when suddenly I hear Courtney's voice.

"Ron, wait!" she yells.

I stop the car and see Courtney running toward me, down the neglected driveway.

Now what?

She reaches me as I roll down the window. "Everything okay?" I ask.

"You're not going to believe this," she says, sounding annoyed, not panicked.

"What? What is it?"

"She's not home."

"Okay…"

"And I don't have a key because I slipped it in my wallet."

"Ah."

"I'm sorry. I must be like the biggest pain in the ass ever."

"I wouldn't say *ever*, but you're certainly working your way up there." I wink.

Lightning flashes in the sky. We both look up. Thunder rumbles.

"So what do you want to do?" I ask. "Do you think she'll be home soon? Should we wait for her?"

"I doubt she'll be home anytime soon, honestly. She's out with her boyfriend, which means she'll probably come back pretty late, if at all. Most of the time she winds up sleeping there and returning the next morning."

"I see."

"Yeah... So... What do you think? I could come back to your place for a while. Hang out."

"No, that's not going to work," I say quickly.

"Why not?" she asks, her bottom lip forming a slight pout.

"Because it won't fly with my wife, at all. I can't just bring some random gorgeous woman home with me."

She smiles at the compliment. It starts to rain. "Please," she says. "Are you sure she'll mind?"

"I'm afraid so. Ordinarily, I might get away with it, but the thing is, I kind of made a stupid mistake earlier and told her that you were a man."

"Why on Earth did you do that?"

"Because I didn't want her to get jealous. You know how wives get."

"No, actually, I don't," she says, looking annoyed again.

"You know what I mean. Look..." I stare into her pleading eyes and feel my resolve wavering. The rain picks up and pours down on her. She looks like an abandoned puppy. "All right, just get in here and get out of the rain, for crying out loud. We'll figure something out."

She grins and runs around to the other side. By the time she's back inside the car, her hair and clothes are drenched; the outline of her bra now visible through her low-cut, wet blouse. "Woo! That rain is crazy. You got a towel?"

I look at her.

"Kidding," she says.

"Wait, I do have this," I say. I grab a napkin from inside the middle console and hand it to her. She thanks me and uses it to dry her face and hands. She runs her hands through her hair several times, playfully flicking tiny droplets of water at my face.

"So, have you decided what you want to do with me yet?" She smirks.

I shake my head. "You're trouble, you know that?"

"Am not."

I run my hands through my own hair a couple times, trying to control the joyful anxiety that's building inside. "All right, let me think about this for a second."

She perks up and grabs ahold of my arm. "Hey! We should stop and get a drink somewhere."

"Eh... Sounds good in theory, but..."

"Come on, it'll be fun. I could sure use a drink, couldn't you?"

"I could, yes. A drink sounds amazing right about now. I just can't. I need to get home for dinner. I'm already late. It wouldn't be right."

She slumps her shoulders. "All right."

"Sorry," I say.

Water drips from her hair and runs down her chest, disappearing beneath her clothes. She glances out the window into the downpour.

"Well, I guess you could drop me off at the nearest park bench. I can sleep there for the night. Better than nothing, I suppose."

I shake my head. "Yeah, sure."

"Do you have any extra newspapers I could use to stay warm?"

"Don't be ridiculous. Don't you have any other friends you can stay with?"

She shakes her head. "Nope."

I give her a look.

"I'm serious," she says.

"You have one friend?"

"That lives nearby."

I sigh, loud and firm. "Fine, what about a hotel? There's a bunch around here."

"I would, but how am I going to pay for a room without my purse?"

"Right."

"But, hey, if you're offering to pay…"

A series of images race through my mind. First, I picture myself standing there with her in the hotel lobby, paying for the room. Then, walking her to the door and agreeing to stay and chat for a few minutes. Next we're sitting on the edge of the bed, talking and laughing, scooting closer and closer to each other… But it all fades away as I picture Kate reading through the credit card statement a few days later, her eyes going wide with rage as she spots the hotel charge.

"I could pay you back," she says.

"Nope, that won't work either."

"How come? You broke?"

"No, I have money, but I'd have to use a credit card and Kate handles all the finances. She'd see it on the bank statement. I'd be screwed. She'd never believe that I didn't sleep there with you."

"Oh..." she says, like the idea of us sleeping together is a brand new concept. Like the thought that Kate might consider that is completely foreign to her. Or perhaps just the idea of sleeping with me is foreign. "But as far as your wife knows, I'm a man, remember?"

I look at her.

"So she'll have no reason to think you stayed there with me."

"That's a good point..."

She smiles.

"No, it's still a bad idea."

Her smile vanishes.

"She'll figure it out, somehow. Trust me, nothing good will come of it, unless I'm looking for the quickest route to divorce."

"Are you?" she asks.

I stare out my window, through a thousand tiny water droplets. They're all making their way down the window, slowly losing their fight against gravity. Some more than others.

Courtney scoots closer and puts her hand on my leg. "I got another idea."

"What is it?"

"I'll ride back with you to your house, but I won't go inside."

"Where will you go? I ask.

"Nowhere. I'll stay right here in your car until morning."

I laugh. "Good one."

"No, I'm serious. Hear me out for a sec. I'll lay down on your back seat and sleep there for the night. Your wife will never even know I'm here. Then, when you leave for work in the morning, you can drop me back off on your way out. I'm sure my friend will be home by then. It'll be perfect. It's fool-proof. What do you say?"

"I say...you're crazy."

She tilts her head, her eyes conveying a strong level of disappointment and impatience.

"Even if we don't get caught, I still won't feel right about leaving you outside all night. It's bound to get cold and uncomfortable."

"Nonsense, I'll be fine. I can rough it for one night. At least I'll have a roof over my head."

"Still, it seems a bit absurd."

She shrugs. "Maybe a little. But honestly, what other choice do I have at this point?"

I pause to rethink the whole scenario. Certainly, there are other options out there. I could drop her off at any local bar. I'm sure there'd be a number of men willing to help her out. But what if it was someone dangerous? What if she puts her trust in the wrong person and gets hurt? Or killed? I can see it now... I'll read the morning paper and see an article on the front page titled "Woman Found Dead in a Ditch off the Side of the Road. Witnesses Say She Was Last Seen Leaving a Bar with an Unidentified Male." Unlikely, of course. But possible. I'd never forgive myself.

I look at her. She's staring at me expectantly, her eyes full of hope.

"You know what?" I say. "This plan of yours is so ridiculous, it might actually work."

"Sweet!" She claps her hands together in celebration. "I knew you'd come around."

I flash a crooked smile. "I can't believe you're actually excited about this. *Why* are you excited about this?"

She shrugs. "Nothing wrong with allowing a little excitement to leak into our ordinary lives every once in a while, right?"

"Right, but it's the exciting part I'm confused by. What about sleeping in my car is exciting to you?"

"I don't know…" She stares off to the side. "Because it's dangerous, I suppose."

"The only real danger I see is my wife finding you."

"Well, there you go!" she says. "Sounds dangerous enough for me."

"And you're happy about that?"

"Not happy, exactly. It just… It makes me feel like a kid again. You know? Like I'm twelve years old, snooping through my mother's bedside table drawer for loose change. Trying to steal as much as I can before she catches me."

"If you say so."

I pull back onto the road and drive.

I suppose she's right. Danger *is* part of the appeal, even if it does result in my early demise.

As we get closer to the highway, I notice a bar ahead called Kelly's Pub.

"Ooh, let's go there," Courtney says, perking up with excitement once again.

"I told you, I'm in a time crunch."

"Blah, blah, blah. Come on, when was the last time you did something spontaneous?"

"No idea."

"Exactly."

"I'm going home."

She sighs. "Well, can you at least stop and let me use the bathroom real quick?"

I look at her.

"What? I need to go," she says.

"You can't hold it for like ten more minutes?"

"And then what? Pee on your front lawn?"

"Crap, you're right. Good point."

"I mean I will if I have to, but…"

I hold my hand in the air. "Nope. Say no more. I'm stopping." I pull into the parking lot and park right in front. Guilt worms through my gut as I glance nervously at the time displayed on the dashboard.

"Thank you! Be right back." She exits the car.

I lean forward against the steering wheel with my face in my hands, wondering what the hell I've gotten myself into. She's really going to sleep in my car. I must be insane. Maybe I *should* have taken my chances with the hotel idea. Can this day get any stranger? The term 'stranger danger' passes through my mind.

I picture Kate walking outside and discovering Courtney in the morning. How would I possibly explain that? I'd have to tell her the truth. I'd never hear the end of it. She'd never trust me again.

I could drive away right now and leave Courtney here. I'm sure she'll be fine. She'll get a ride from some charming single guy who will gladly take her home and be free to take her inside his house. Into his bed. I'd be doing her a favor.

I lift my head and glance around. I grab ahold of the shift stick, prepared and ready to drive away, but hesitate once again as I imagine myself running into Courtney on the train next week. She'll scowl when she sees me. "Oh, look, if it isn't the asshole who left me for dead in the middle of nowhere."

The passenger-side door swings open, startling me. Courtney pops into the car with a full shot glass in each hand.

"What's this?" I ask.

"Whiskey!"

"You're something else, you know that?"

"Thank you."

"How did you manage that without any money?"

"I can be very persuasive."

"Yeah, no shit."

She hands me a glass. "Here you go."

"Thanks." I take it from her. "You're insane. You know that, right?"

"All the best people are." She raises her glass, "Cheers, to new beginnings."

I raise my glass. "New beginnings..." We tap our glasses and drink. It's much stronger than I anticipated. I do my best to hide my shock as the fiery liquid burns its way down my throat.

She swallows and scrunches her eyelids shut. "Woo-wee!" she howls. She looks at me with watery eyes. "Not bad. It's got some kick."

"That it does," I say. I don't drink often, so I already feel it warming my chest, relaxing me.

"So..." She sets her glass down in the center cup holder. "What now, Ronald McDonald?"

I snicker.

She smiles, and it lights up her face, warming my insides even more than the alcohol. I can't help but observe how beautiful she is again, both inside and out. I'm glad she's still here with me. Sure this whole thing is crazy. Sure it might all end in disaster. But you know what? I'm having fun. I haven't felt good in months. Maybe years. I think it's worth it. God, I hope it's worth it.

Her eyes wander past me, out the window, and her eyes widen again. "Oh my God, come see this!"

"I really think we should—"

"It'll only take a second, come on." She gets out, runs around to my side of the car, and pulls on the handle of my door with great enthusiasm. The door doesn't open of course, and she falls back and lands hard on the ground. I instinctively try to open the door myself to get out but am met with the same resistance. "Oh, for the love of…" I crawl across the car and exit out the other side for what feels like the slowest rescue attempt of all time. When I finally reach her, she's already sitting up.

I kneel down beside her and place my hand on her back. "Are you okay?"

She rubs her eyes for a few seconds, then she looks at me and smiles. "Yeah. I'm good."

"Sorry about that. It seems that door no longer opens."

She brushes off her arms. "First your car tries to deafen me, and now it's tossing me on the ground. Are there any other tricks up its sleeve that I should prepare for?"

"No, I think that's it." I grab her hands and pull her up off the ground.

"Thank you, sir." She brushes the dirt off her butt and smirks.

I smile back.

"Come on," she says. She takes my hand and leads me across the parking lot where we stand together by the side of the road, looking up at the sky. Somehow, like magic, the rain has stopped, and the sky has cleared up just enough to make the moon visible. It's big and bright and full of hope.

She loops her arm through mine. "It's beautiful, isn't it?"

"It sure is."

"This weather is something else. It's as if it can't decide what it wants to do."

Tiny stars surround the moon, their dim lights vying for our attention. Despite being next to the road, the atmosphere is quiet and peaceful, like the world is on pause so we can enjoy the moment.

Courtney speaks into the silence. "I know we can't see much right now, but I always find it relaxing to lie down or stand still while studying the sky."

The Satellite Restaurant appears in my mind. Sitting there with Kate. "Never done much stargazing myself, but I like the idea of it."

I sense her looking at me, then suddenly she kisses my cheek and squeezes my arm tight.

"What's that for?" I ask.

"Just saying thanks for tonight. You're the best company I've had in a while."

"You're welcome. Same here, actually. It's been a rough week so far. I needed this…"

"I hear you. Hell, under different circumstances, I'd say this was the best first date I've ever been on."

We both laugh nervously, and then share a moment, locked in each other's eyes, savoring the endless unspoken possibilities that are trying their hardest to fill the space between us. The alcohol continues to work on me, mellowing me out. Every-thing feels perfect. Too perfect. That's probably why it's not real. Just a temporary fantasy. A short-lived alternate reality.

She rests her head against my shoulder as we continue gaz-ing at the one beautifully clear section of the night sky.

"When I was eleven, I asked my parents for a telescope for Christmas," she says. "It seemed like such a cool idea. I thought I would discover new planets. Maybe even become famous do-ing it."

"Sounds like an ambitious goal. Did you get it?"

"Yep. No thanks to my father, though. He said it was too expensive. Still, I held out hope that Santa would come through for me, since cost wasn't a factor for him. So I waited and got it after all." She lifts her head off my shoulder and looks at me, her eyes distant, like the memory is running rampant through her head and she's right there with it. "I found out years later that it was my mom's doing. She arranged it behind my father's back. She even sold some of her favorite jewelry to get it. An-yway, it was the only thing I got that year because my mom couldn't afford anything else, and my father couldn't care less. I was so focused on that telescope, I didn't even notice it was the only gift I got. I ran right up to my bedroom with it. First came the challenge of trying to put it together on my own, which was awful, by the way. There were so many pieces, and the instructions were definitely not written for a child. I felt un-qualified for a job that I couldn't rely on anyone else to do."

I suddenly remember the oversized coat that I had spotted in her car. Seems strange that the father she's describing now would give her a coat like that to keep her warm.

"But eventually, I finished putting it together. I stuck it in front of my bedroom window and pointed it right up at the sky, ready for my first discovery."

She pauses.

"Well? What did you find?" I ask.

She takes a few more seconds to answer. "I found that I didn't know what the hell I was looking at. It was a confusing mess, just like I was."

I recall how she referred to herself as a mess earlier, as well.

"I could never get the focus quite right. Even when I did, I still wasn't sure what I was looking at. I wanted to ask for help but couldn't bring myself to. I knew my dad would be annoyed, and my mom already had enough on her plate. I didn't want to bother her with my problems or seem ungrateful."

She glances up at the moon again. "But I stuck with it. I decided I needed to at least learn the basics if I was going to discover anything. Eventually, I started recording my observations in a drawing pad, and then I would wait for my dad to leave and go to the bar in the evenings, and I would show my mom what I drew and ask her what she thought. I asked her if she knew what any of it was. But she never did. She always felt bad about it too—I could tell by the way she said it—so I would do my best to hide my disappointment. Then one day, after about the second week of drawing these pictures, I went to her with my latest discovery. At first, she shook her head like usual. But as I turned to walk away, she called my name. You know what she said to me?"

I shake my head.

"She told me she'd figured it out. She said the reason she never knew which planets they were was because I was the first to discover them. They were brand new. And just like that, my dream came true. It made all the difference in the world. She even helped me name them." Courtney runs her hands through her hair a couple times. "Long story short, neither of us knew what to do with this discovery, or who to show it to, so we decided to keep it to ourselves. It would be our little secret, just the two of us with our own little universe."

I smile. "Sounds like a nice memory."

"It is," she nods. "It was short-lived, though. Not long after, I hit puberty and became far too impatient for stargazing. I threw our book of planets in the closet to collect dust, and that was the end of that. Then I learned that my father was screwing some skank on the side. Every time he left to go to the bar, he was also seeing her."

"Damn."

"My parents got divorced and shared joint custody of me. I viewed it similarly to the difference between heaven and hell."

"I'm sorry," I say, noticing the subtle change in her tone.

I think of my own kids. How would they handle a divorce?

Courtney sniffs. "It's okay. Anyway, I only mention it because, soon after the divorce, I went and pulled that book back out of the closet and placed it prominently back on my favorite shelf. By then I'd figured out that it was all bullshit—giving the stars different names and stories doesn't change what they really are. But it still made me feel better. So I kept it close and would look through it whenever things got bad. Particularly when I went to visit my father in his creepy little run down shack he called home."

I picture Courtney's friend's house, shrouded with vines and darkness.

"I take it you're still not too close with your dad."

"No. I hate him." She pauses. "He's a creep."

The jacket in Courtney's car enters my mind again.

"I still have the book, you know?"

"You do?"

"Yup. Old habits die hard, I guess. Still, to this day, every once in a while, I'll pick a page at random and look at the name Mom had me write down, and I'll feel better. Every time." She looks at me. "I've never told anyone that before."

I smile.

We start walking back to the car.

"You should take it somewhere," I say. "You know, to get a second opinion. You never know?"

She flashes a crooked smile. "You're sweet, but I stopped believing in fairy tales a long time ago."

"I'm sure you've thought about it before, though, right?"

She stops walking, and I stop with her. "Thought about it? Sure. Would I? Not a chance. I want it to cheer me up, not make me look like a fool."

"Right," I say.

"Besides, as you're probably aware, when it comes to fantasy vs. reality, fantasy tends to be the more enjoyable choice."

I look into her eyes, feeling the longing bubbling up again.

"We'd better get going," she says. "Your dinner's getting cold."

We continue walking toward the car, our arms no longer looped together. Sadness hangs in the air above us, spreading down and swelling in my chest like I've lost something near and dear to me. I wonder if that's how she feels too.

"Still have that telescope?" I ask.

"Nah. Sold it to help pay for college."

"Maybe I can read your book sometime," I say.

"Thanks, but I doubt it." She looks at me, her gaze dreamy, but critical. Held back by the restraints of reality.

We stop at the car door. She's studying the sky again, only now the moon has vanished, and the dark clouds have returned. The rain is not finished with us yet.

"Are you happy, Ron?"

"Uh…sure." Her direct question jars me a bit. "I mean, as much as anyone else." I hope that wasn't as unconvincing as it sounded. "Why do you ask?"

She pulls her eyes away from the sky and looks at me. "Because you don't seem happy."

"I don't?"

She shakes her head slowly. "Nope."

A man and a woman burst through the front door of the bar, clinging to each other and laughing hysterically, no doubt intoxicated. Courtney and I watch them as they kiss before getting inside their car and driving away.

"Well… I guess I'm not *that* happy."

Her mouth curves upwards into a sympathetic, but sad smile.

"I wonder if love ever truly lasts?" she asks.

"I think it can. My parents are still happily married. Forty-two years and still going strong."

"Maybe I can meet them someday," she says.

The sound of thunder arrives and spreads quietly in the distance. She looks up toward the sky again. The clouds are condensing, getting darker and more ominous by the second.

"It doesn't look good," she says. "Aren't you glad you stopped to enjoy the view while you had the chance?"

I open the passenger side door.

Courtney holds her hand out. "After you."

We get back on the highway. It's quiet in the car. Courtney stares out her window, resting her chin on her fist. Rain begins pounding away at the windshield. I turn the wipers on and glance at the clock. I should have been home an hour ago.

"You're really late, huh?" she asks.

"Yeah, sort of. It's okay, though."

"Sorry, I'm the worst." Her tone is sincere. A tad regretful, even.

I roll my eyes. "You're far from the worst. Shit happens. Don't worry about it."

"You're sweet. How come I never meet any single guys like you?"

"I don't know," I say, relieved the mood is lightening up again.

"I swear, the good ones are all married already. It's not fair. Maybe I'm just destined to be alone forever."

"Please. Women like you are never alone forever, unless you want to be."

"What's that supposed to mean?"

"You know exactly what I mean. Look at you. You're gorgeous. You're smart, caring, successful... Most guys would kill to be with a girl like you."

My palms feel moist against the steering wheel, and my hands tremble in anticipation of her response. But she doesn't say anything, which makes me even more nervous. I glance at her and see that she's once again staring through her window at the darkness. The occasional passing streetlight reveals rose-colored cheeks and a handful of lost dreams behind her wet eyes.

I took it too far.

"How old are you, anyway?" I ask, attempting to kill the silence and move things along.

She hesitates before answering, twirling the ends of her hair with her fingers. "Twenty-eight."

I snicker. "Yeah, you've still got plenty of time."

"If you say so."

"You do, trust me."

"You act like you're an old man or something, and your life is almost over. You're practically the same age as me."

"For what it's worth, I feel younger and younger with each passing moment I spend with you."

Her mouth forms another small, sad smile. She sets her hand down on my leg. My heart speeds up, and suddenly I'm gripping the steering wheel with white knuckles, aware that I've definitely said too much and am steering things in the wrong direction.

I pull onto an off-ramp and exit the highway. Almost home, finally. It feels like I've been driving all night without actually getting anywhere.

"I still feel bad about this, you know? It's too bad I can't just sneak you into my guest room." I smirk.

"Then why don't you?" she asks.

Sweat builds on my palms again. "Well, because…it would be too difficult, for one. Too risky. Kate would probably find you. Trust me, she never misses anything out of the ordinary. If I move the couch an inch to the left, she—"

"Ron."

"Yeah?"

"Relax, I was kidding."

"Right. I knew that."

"It's better this way, anyway," she says. "Like you said, you don't know me, and I don't know you. I could be a serial killer."

"There's always *that* possibility..." Then it occurs to me for the first time: she *could* be dangerous. Why haven't I even considered this?

We pull into the driveway of my white Victorian home. It's not a *bad* house by any means. The first time Kate and I pulled up to this four-bedroom, two-and-a-half bath house with the fenced-in backyard, Kate made a pun about the vinyl siding. "Vinyl you power-wash my sides someday?" she said and curved herself seductively toward me as we stood considering it. I responded without hesitation. "Wooden't you know it, it's vinylly our house!" It's a fine house, but we never intended to live in it for so long. It was supposed to be a starter home. These days I find myself hoping this is just a starter life.

"Well, here we are," I say. "Now we just have to hope and pray that my wife doesn't find a reason to go into my car tonight."

"Don't worry; even if she does, I'll just tell her I'm homeless and needed a place to sleep."

"Yeah, because that's believable. I'm sure you'd pass for a homeless person with your fancy business attire, diamond earrings, and high heels."

"Perhaps it would be more convincing if I took my clothes off." She grins.

"Funny. She's not going to come out here, especially not in this weather. So keep your clothes on, Lady Godiva. For now, at least..."

She raises her eyebrows.

"Joke," I say. "Are you hungry?"

"Not really. I can wait until tomorrow."

"Don't be silly, you can't go all night without dinner. I'll find something and bring it out to you."

"If you insist. But seriously, don't get yourself in trouble for my sake. I'll feel really bad after all you've done for me."

"I insist."

She leans in and kisses my cheek again, slow to pull away. When she finally does, her eyes latch onto mine and hypnotize me, burrowing deep into my brain. "Thanks, Ron."

"No problem..." I respond, suddenly dazed. "See you in a bit."

She crawls into the back seat and pops back up holding Kate's coat in the air. My heart accelerates. She studies it curiously for a moment before extending her arm for me to take it, her eyes appearing both sad and innocent. I reach over and grab it from her, struck with a sudden overwhelming sensation that I've done something terribly wrong. I know it's just a coat, but the sight of Courtney holding it makes me feel as though their paths have already crossed, or that they're destined to cross eventually, and now there's no turning back. Danger looms around every corner.

Panicked, I grab hold of the door handle and pray that it acts accordingly. I give it a good pull. Nothing, as expected. I pull it again, more viciously this time, while slamming my body against it repeatedly. After about the fifth slam, the handle breaks off of the door. I stare at it, then look at Courtney, who's throwing me a blank stare.

"Oops," I say, and slide across the seats to exit the car. I toss the coat in the trunk, hiding it like a dirty secret. Then I open the back doors and watch as Courtney stretches herself out along the seat, trying to get comfortable. I take my own jacket off and hand it to her. "Here, keep this. Not sure how cold it's going to get tonight."

"Thanks." She takes it from me and pins it to her chest. "I'm sure it will come in handy."

I nod, unable to take my eyes off her.

"Something else you want to say?" she asks.

I shake my head, tapping my hand against the roof, ready to go inside, but my mind is running nervously. "How will you let me know if you need me? You don't even have a phone." I realize I'm starting to sound like a father.

"I'm sure I'll manage. I'm not a child, after all."

"Right. Sorry…"

She's right. It's like deep down I want to take care of her, like she's a homeless kitten or something. But why? Maybe to fill some strange void in me I didn't know was there until today.

I close the door and take my time ascending the front steps of my home, pondering the many directions this night could go. My shadow lengthens with each step, then disappears once I reach the door.

CHAPTER EIGHT

HOME SWEET HOME

Kate is inside washing dishes. My dinner awaits me on the kitchen table, wrapped in plastic.

"Hey, hon," I say.

"Hey." She glances at me. "Finally made it, huh?"

"No, it's just your imagination."

"What's that?" she yells, trying to hear me over the running water.

"Yes, I made it."

"Took you long enough. Did you get your new friend home okay?"

"Yup."

"Your dinner's on the table. I had to eat without you," she pouts. "I was hungry."

"It's okay. Sorry it took so long."

"Where does he live? Afghanistan?"

"Might as well have."

"Did you get caught up in that storm?"

"Yeah, it was coming down pretty good." I picture Courtney standing in the rain and feel a sudden desire to return to her, then immediately hate myself for it.

"Supposably, it's going to get worse before the night is over." She grabs the last of the dinner pans and scrubs it with a brush. "Did the guy make any comments about your car?" She smirks.

"No, why would he?"

"Oh, I don't know. Perhaps he noticed how…peachy it is?"

"He didn't. He noticed how orange it is."

She chuckles.

"He thought it was a cool car."

"Sure he did. I suppose he loved your stereo system as well." We eye each other with playful tension. "Okay, I'll stop," she says. "I know how much you love your car. It was nice of you to help a stranger like that."

I shrug. "Yeah, I guess."

"What?" she yells.

"Yeah, I guess it was!" I repeat louder.

"Why are you yelling?"

My headache from this morning creeps its way back in. "Can we talk after you're done with that, please?"

She turns the water off. "How was work?"

"It was all right. I'm not feeling too great, though. I've got a pretty bad headache."

"Did you take something for it?"

"Yeah, you could say that. How was your day?"

"Fine," she says. She looks at my head. "What happened to your forehead?"

"Oh…" If I tell her the truth, she'll most definitely go outside to view the damage. "It's nothing. I bumped it on the hood of that guy's car."

She squints with confusion.

"I offered to look at the engine first. You know...to see if I could help find the problem." I try to keep a serious face.

Kate laughs. Then she covers her mouth with her hand. "I'm sorry. You? Under the hood of a car?"

"Yeah, I know."

"That was your first mistake."

"Hey!" I say, pointing my finger at her. "I found something, I'll have you know."

"And what was that?"

"Jack."

She snickers. "Shocker. And yet, you still managed to hurt yourself."

"Yeah," I say, feeling the bump.

She pulls my hand away from my head. "Stop touching it, you're gonna make it worse." She moves my bangs to the side. "Let me look."

I sigh.

"Stop moving." She studies the bump closely for a moment and then turns my head sideways. "Get in the light so I can see it better."

I sigh again, louder this time. "You're so bossy."

"Don't be such a baby. You know you love me."

"Mm-hmm."

"Wow," she says.

Uh-oh. It must be worse than I thought. "What? What is it?" I ask.

"Your gray hair really shows in this light."

"Gee, thanks."

"It's nothing to be ashamed of, dear."

"Are you done examining me yet, doctor? Can we be done with this?"

"Just hold still." She stands up on the tips of her toes to get a better look, pressing her chest against mine and practically knocking me over. I smile and wrap one arm around her for support. I keep her held there, tight against me, enjoying the closeness. I study her face lovingly. My eyes fall upon her lips and stay there.

"It's all swollen," she says.

I lean into her, suddenly unable to resist the urge to kiss her.

"Does it hurt when I touch it?" She presses her finger against the wound.

I feel a sharp sting and flinch.

"Yes, it does," I say, annoyed. I rub my forehead gently to soothe it.

She lowers her hands and takes a step back, her worry crease forming between her eyes, looking at me like she's still mulling the situation over in her head. "Well, no wonder you have a headache."

I nod.

"You did connect the two, right?"

"Yes, Kate."

"Just checking. Never can tell with you."

The home phone rings and startles us.

"I got it," says Kate. She moves past me and grabs the phone off the wall. "Hello? Hey there." Silence. "Yup. Sure did." Silence. "Hmm." Her eyes connect with mine. "It appears so, yes." She turns her back toward me, facing the wall. "So far. Yup, I'm good. Okay. Talk to you tomorrow." She hangs up. "Come on," she says to me. "Help me dry off the dishes."

Kate heads to the sink, humming to herself. I follow her over there and stare at her. She hands me a dish to put away.

I set it inside the cabinet. "Well?"

"Well what?" she asks, her forehead crinkled with confusion.

"What do you mean, *well what*?" I ask. "You really don't know why I'm looking at you?"

She shrugs. "Because you think I'm beautiful?"

"Who was on the phone, Kate?"

"Oooh... It was just Kay from work."

"Kay?"

She nods. "Mm-hmm."

"What'd she want?"

"She called to warn me about a client I have tomorrow. Apparently he's an asshole." She hands me another dish. "I can't escape them this week. Did I tell you about the guy I met with yesterday?"

I shake my head and put the dish away, wondering if I'm one of the assholes she's referring to.

"We were looking at a six hundred thousand dollar house, and this guy had the nerve to request that the seller drop the price to two hundred."

"You don't say?"

"Unbelievable!" She hands me another dish. "Some creep who just left his wife. He's shopping for a place of his own, but he can't afford a high payment, because of all the child support he has to pay now."

"No doubt."

"Yeah. I bet you a million dollars he got caught cheating, too. And now he's trying to move in with his mistress. He seemed like the type. I mean, why else would he walk out on his marriage after all those years?"

"I can't imagine," I say.

"Exactly. I'm sure he had it made already, too. Good job, cozy home, loving wife, healthy children. Some people are so ignorant…"

"You sure know an awful lot about this guy's personal life. Are you sure *you're* not the mistress?"

She gives me a look. "Yeah, because I have time for an affair." She hands me another dish. "Trust me, if I did, I probably would be."

I nod. "Cute."

"Kidding, obviously."

Obviously, especially since her sex drive died months ago.

"Stop that," says Kate.

"Stop what?"

"You know what. I see what you're thinking right now."

"You do?"

"Mm-hmm. Sure do. Don't appreciate it, either."

"What am I thinking?"

"That I'd make a lousy mistress."

I smirk. "And why would I think that?"

"Because all I do is bitch and moan and never want to have sex."

"Your words, not mine."

She considers it for another moment, then sighs loudly. "Hell, who am I kidding? I would make an awful mistress." She laughs.

I laugh. "The worst." It feels great to laugh together. I haven't seen her this relaxed in weeks.

She leans forward and kisses me softly. Then, as she looks into my eyes, a lingering hint of what once was hangs upon us in the air like a noose. "Anyway," she says. "I can't imagine how heartbroken his wife must be." She hands me the last dish.

"Stuck with two kids, while he goes off to relive his twenties. Disgusting."

"I can see you feel strongly about this," I say. I put the dish away and close the cabinet door.

She steps closer. "I'd be furious."

I step back. "I have no doubt."

She takes another step forward, and I fight the urge to retreat. "Like, blood on the carpet furious."

I picture Courtney inside my car. The way she looked with her wet hair. The light in her eyes. Her warm breath against my skin.

Thunder roars outside and rattles the walls. I swallow. "Good to know."

Kate places her hands on her hips. "I'm serious, Ron. Don't let me catch you cheating with some blonde Barbie. It will not end well for you."

"Define 'cheating,'" I say.

She narrows her eyes. "It's not an appropriate time for jokes."

I chuckle nervously. "What? I'm just asking. I think it's important I understand the rules if my life is going to be on the line."

"Loving or caring for another woman in an inappropriate manner."

"What about men?"

"Inappropriate, meaning emotionally or physically. Especially emotionally."

"Especially? I always thought—"

"I'll kill her, Ron."

"All right, I get it. Duly noted. But you have nothing to worry about." I place my hand on her arm. "I don't love anyone else. Physically or emotionally. Barbie doll or otherwise."

"Good." She raises her chin in a self-righteous manner. "So, that was the highlight of my week so far. How did your meeting go today?"

"Meeting?"

"Yeah. The one you've been stressing about?"

"Oh, right... It went fine. I think..." I know I attended a meeting today, but I can't remember anything about it.

She nods. "Fascinating. Well, I think I'll run upstairs and take a quick shower and get ready for bed." She places her hands on my chest. "And...if you're not too tired, maybe we can snuggle up in bed. Talk. See what happens..."

I smile. "Yeah, sounds great."

She kisses me again. "Don't forget to eat your dinner."

"I won't."

She snaps her fingers. "Shoot, that reminds me... I left my black coat in your car yesterday. I'm gonna grab it real quick; it's supposed to be colder tomorrow." She heads to the hallway.

After a slight delay, due to the fact that Courtney had escaped my mind completely over the course of the last ten minutes, the reality of what Kate's doing hits me like a sledgehammer. "Kate! Wait!" I run toward her.

Why didn't I bring that stupid thing inside when I had the chance?

I reach her right as she's grabbing her yellow rain jacket off the hook.

"Yeah?"

"Uh..." I say, trying to catch my breath. "Don't worry about it... I'll get it for you."

"It's fine. I got it. It'll only take a second." She slips her arms through the squeaky sleeves.

I grab her shoulder, my chest bursting with anxiety. "No, really. I got it. You shouldn't be outside in this nasty weather. You'll get drenched. You might even catch a cold. Plus, I have to go out there, anyway."

"What for?"

"I left my wallet in there by accident."

"Oh."

I wait, praying I'm in the clear.

"Well, I hope you locked your car," she says.

"I did." The tension dissipates.

"Cool." She pulls the zipper up on her jacket. "Then, I'll grab it for you while I'm out there." She flips her hood up over her head.

"No! You can't!" I yell.

She raises her eyebrows.

"Please don't go outside," I say in a calmer tone.

"All right, Ron. What the hell is going on?"

"Nothing," I say.

"There's obviously something you're not telling me. Now, cough it up."

I put my head down.

"Either tell me what you're hiding in your car, or I'm going out there to find out for myself."

I put my hand up. "Okay, I'll tell you."

She shifts her stance, resting one hand on her hip.

"The thing is... I have something in there I don't want you to see."

She gives me a couple of heavy blinks.

"Because..."

She leans her head forward.

The wheel is spinning again. Our anniversary flashes through my mind. "Because it would ruin the surprise." I smile.

Her face loosens up, and the corners of her mouth turn upwards. "Oh, really?"

"Yes. And—"

She covers my mouth with her hand. "Shh... Say no more. I understand. And I love you. So much."

She gives me a long, hard kiss. Then she peers into my eyes, all sweet and dangerous, like a tiger who's up to no good. Similar to the way she used to look at me back when we first got married. Similar to the way Courtney looked at me right before she climbed into my back seat. "I'll be upstairs." Kate slips her rain jacket back off, hangs it on the hook, and goes upstairs.

I slump back against the wall, breathing a hard sigh of relief. Yet I don't feel much better. Here I am worrying about Courtney, trying to keep her safe and protected from Kate. Meanwhile, Kate's busy being affectionate for the first time in centuries. And now I've lied to her again to avoid inevitable disaster. On the eve of our anniversary, no less.

Our anniversary. Damn... It's the first time I've thought of it since this morning. And it was to help me tell a lie. I never got her a gift on my way home either! Too busy doting on Courtney to remember. What does that say about me?

I still have time to make this right. I haven't done anything irredeemable yet. Nothing I can't fix.

First things first. I'm going to bring Courtney a plate of food and then she should be good for the night. Then I can concentrate on Kate. I'll join her upstairs, and we can make love like rock stars. Then, tomorrow night, when Courtney's safely out of my life, I'll take Kate out to dinner to celebrate our anniversary. It'll be perfect.

I grab my dinner plate from the table and look at it. It's dingy and made of hard plastic, with a faded floral design flowing around the edges. Part of an old set that Kate bought for the house many years ago, just before we moved in. She was glowing with excitement and new life the day she brought them home to our tiny apartment. She was seven months pregnant with an adorably round belly. I was sitting at the kitchen table, budgeting our finances and trying not to pull my hair out while attempting to figure out how we could afford this house. "What do you think?" she asked, presenting them to me. "They'll match the wallpaper in the new kitchen perfectly." She was right about the wallpaper. Today there's nothing left that matches the plate. A few years ago we tore all of the wallpaper down and covered the walls in tan-colored paint instead. One of our many desperate attempts at change.

When we ate our first meals at our first home together, we used these plates. It was a happy time. Over the years we'd bought proper dinner plates, and these were relegated to the kids. And now this is the only one we have left from the set, the others being lost or broken.

Looking at it now, it reminds me of a rare innocence. Once it's gone, it doesn't come back. And now I'm using it to feed another woman. A deep longing seeps through my stomach and stirs around, motivating me now to hurry up and get upstairs to Kate.

I walk outside with the plate. Struggling to see through the pounding rain, I glance up at our dimly lit bedroom window to make sure Kate isn't standing there, watching. She's not. I hop into the passenger seat and find Courtney lying in the back seat, fiddling with her gold bracelet.

"That was fast," she says.

"I wanted to make sure you ate something."

She looks at the plate. "Oh, nice! Chicken and mashed potatoes, my favorite."

"Is it really?"

"Hell yeah!" She grabs the plate from my hand.

Courtney is irresistibly full of life. I can't remember the last time Kate reacted to anything with such enthusiasm. I miss it. Thinking about it now, it occurs to me that I'm one of the things dragging her down.

I picture the days when we were young and in love. She had a collection of lion-themed clothes and knick-knacks, including a lion poster hanging in her college dorm room. We discussed art and philosophy. We flipped through photo albums, sharing our hopes and dreams for the future until the sun came up. There was no one else in this world, except for her.

And now... My eyes run a marathon over Courtney's body. ...*This*.

"I'd better get back inside. I'll come back later for your plate if I can."

She flashes a warm smile. "You spoil me too much."

"I do?"

She nods. "Mm-hm. I don't mind, though. It's quite flattering. Your wife's a lucky woman." She pulls her knees up to her chest and hugs her legs.

My eyes stay glued to hers. It takes several seconds for me to tear them away. "It's no problem... I'll see you in the morning."

I force myself out of the car, grab Kate's coat from the trunk and slam it shut. As it occurs to me that I should have been quieter about it, I see the bedroom curtain move. I duck down behind the car. My hands are shaking. This is ridiculous. I'm a criminal outside of my own home.

I peek up to make sure Kate's not there staring down at me and then dash back inside the house. I toss her coat on the hook and grab another plate from the cabinet, hoping there's enough food left over to refill it. But before I even get a chance to check, I hear Kate walking down the stairs. I rush over to the table and take a seat with my empty plate.

She enters the room, drying her hair with a towel. "Finished already?"

"Sure am." Sweat drips down my forehead. Luckily for me, it's raining outside.

"That good, huh?"

I rub my stomach. "Wonderful, thanks. In fact, I'd love more if there is any?"

She gives me a speculative look and glances at the plate. "No, I'm afraid that was the last of it."

"Oh…" I'm unable to hide my disappointment.

"I'm sorry. I thought for sure you'd be full. I gave you a huge plate. You want me to make you something else?"

Does she sense something? A red flag, perhaps. An internal warning, telling her my affections may be drifting elsewhere.

"Nope, not necessary," I say. "Thank you, though."

Her eyebrows furrow, her face full of concern. "You shouldn't eat so fast. It's bad for your digestion."

I nod.

Her hair drying slows to a halt and so does the conversation. "Well… I'll be upstairs, I guess." And up she goes.

My stomach grumbles with hunger. I set the plate back in the cabinet and scarf down a piece of bread, so I'll have something in my stomach.

I pause at the bottom of the stairs, resting my head against the banister.

There's nothing to worry about. Everything is okay. It's been a strange, jacked-up day, but it's all good now. I just need to do the right thing from here on in.

I'm good. Kate's good. Courtney's good. Everything is good.

CHAPTER NINE

EVENING DISCUSSION

I find Kate in bed, reading a book. I lean against the doorframe and watch her, waiting for her to notice me. A moment later our eyes meet, and we both smile.

"Hey," I say, with a quick nod. "What's up?"

She sets the book on her lap, smiling. "Nothing. Relaxing. Waiting for you…"

I strip down to my boxers and head into the bathroom where I find myself staring into the mirror once again, trying to remove Courtney's face from my mind.

Keep your head on straight, Ron. Don't even think about her. She's not real. Kate is real. She loves you, and she's in your bed, waiting for you. Don't say or do anything stupid. Don't screw this up. You're going to crawl into bed with your wife and have sex with her. It's going to be beautiful and amazing and everything else will just fade away.

I take a moment to lean forward and observe my hair, making sure the brown still outweighs the gray. Then I splash a handful of cold water on my face and leave the bathroom.

"Everything okay?" Kate asks.

"Yup. Perfect." I climb into bed and snuggle up close to her, kissing her and caressing her arm.

She puts her hands on my shoulders and pushes me back a little. "Wait. Not yet."

"Why? What's wrong?"

"Nothing's wrong... I'm just not quite ready for you to jump in like that."

"What do you mean?"

She sits up. "I mean, I need a moment." She fidgets, picking at the corners of her fingernails.

"Why are you acting nervous?"

"I'm not," she says, raising her voice.

"Kate, come on, level with me here. What's the matter?"

"I told you, nothing."

"Really? So everything's good? You just don't want to kiss me?"

"No, it's not that." She chews on the corner of her lip. "Just wait a minute, please."

"For what?"

"I don't know. Just talk to me for a little bit."

"Isn't that what we've been doing since I got home?" I ask. She shrugs. "Sort of. But not about anything meaningful."

I sigh and settle down on my side of the bed, worried that talking more will only lead to the demise of my hopes and expectations for the rest of the evening. "All right, Kate. Tell me. What else do I need to talk to you about before I'm allowed to kiss you and be close to you?" She stares at me silently. "You realize we live together, right? We see each other every day. Nobody knows me better than you do. What can I possibly say right now that will come across as new and interesting to you?

Please, help me out, because I'm at a loss. Tell me what you want to hear and I'll say it. Whatever it is."

"Why are you being such a dick about this?"

"I'm not."

"Yes, you are. You're overreacting."

"How so?" I ask.

She narrows her eyes. "You still don't get it, do you?"

I sit up so that our eyes are level, trying to keep things as even as possible. "No, I guess I don't."

"I need more from you, Ron. I want to know what you're thinking and how you're feeling. You don't share yourself with me anymore. Yes, we had fun downstairs, catching up on our days and exchanging witty banter. I enjoyed it. But that's not what I *need* from you."

I stare at her, breathing heavily.

"It's not enough!" she says.

I look down and see her gripping the book, her hands betraying her inner turbulence and whitening from the sheer tension directed at me.

"I don't know what you want from me anymore. But, at this point, I'm pretty sure it's something I'm not capable of giving you."

She huffs and grabs my shoulders. "I'm craving intimacy, Ron. I don't know how to make that any clearer for you."

Again, I'm confused. Wasn't I being intimate when I got into bed and kissed her?

"Kate, it's not like my head is full of all these fantastic ideas that I'm holding back from you. I'm not thinking about anything in particular. Nothing noteworthy, at least. I have a well-established career that I don't plan on changing. So, I go to work and think about work. Then I come home and think about you and the girls and we talk about how our day went. I eat dinner, see what else needs to be done for the night, and put the girls to bed. Then you and I catch up, relax and wind down a bit, hopefully enjoy each other's company for a while, and go to bed. My day is done. I'm afraid that's all I have for you. That's as real as I get."

"And I suppose that's your idea of a perfect day?"

"Hell yeah, it is. If it's drama free and we don't argue... Absolutely. And if, by some miracle, we happen to have sex at the end of it... Best day ever!"

"Well, that's very worrisome to me."

"How so?" I ask.

"So you've already accomplished everything you want to accomplish in this life? You have no further goals beyond what you're already doing? Is that it?"

"Well...I probably wouldn't have worded it quite like that, but yes, more or less."

"Ron, that's depressing!"

"How is it depressing if I'm happy?"

"But you're not happy. I can see it in your face."

"The only thing I'm unhappy about, is you being unhappy with me."

She closes her eyes and takes a breath. "I still want to dream with you, Ron. I want to plan new and exciting things for our future. That right there is a perfect example of something you could talk to me about that I would consider new and interesting."

I massage my eyelids with my fingers, trying to relinquish the stress. "Okay. What else?"

"What else?"

"Yes, what else. Tell me more."

Kate looks away, frustrated.

"Here, I know," I continue. "Let's pretend for a moment that we're living in your perfect world. Here we are in Kate's perfect world, where I'm the perfect husband who says and does all the right things at all the right times and never pisses you off. Are you with me so far?"

She snaps her eyes back to me and glares.

"You should be," I say. "It's a wonderful place to be."

"Sure."

"Okay, good. Now it's your turn. Give me a quick glimpse, from your perspective, of the kind of things I say to you in this world. What kind of thoughts and feelings do I share with you on a daily basis?"

"Anything!" she snaps back at me. "Something pertinent to our lives. Our kids. Us. And it doesn't have to be on a daily basis. Once in a while would be great. You don't share anything with me. You have to be feeling something inside. You're not a robot or a...a goddamn sociopath, *are you?*"

"Of course not! But not everything is meant to be shared with your spouse. Do you really share every single thought you have with me?"

"No, obviously not. That's not what I'm looking for."

"Because you don't want to know all my thoughts."

"What's that supposed to mean?"

"It means exactly what I said."

"Try me," she says.

Courtney enters my mind.

"No way," I say.

"Come on, what are you afraid of? Give me an example and we'll see if I can handle it or not."

I eye her up and down, questioning her motives, while my mind races around for options. I need something that is bad, but not Courtney. "Okay, here's one. Sometimes I hate coming home from work."

"Okay..."

"With the way you've been acting toward me these last few months, there are times when I dread the weekends."

"Fair enough. I can see how you'd feel that way. Sometimes."

"When Fridays come, everyone else I work with is excited to start their weekends. But not me, because I'm too busy worrying about how much attitude I'm going to get from you when I get home."

"All right, I get it," she says sternly.

"What's wrong? I'm just sharing my thoughts."

"Nothing's wrong; there's just no point in talking about this anymore. You're never going to understand where I'm coming from, anyway. Nor do you want to."

"But I do want to. I'm trying like hell to understand. Whether you choose to believe it or not is on you, but I am trying."

"Obviously." Her voice is dry and critical.

I struggle to control the fire kindling in my veins.

We take a few moments to breathe, letting our silence duke it out with the mutual tension.

"Kate, maybe you just need more friends."

"Excuse me?"

"You never spend time with anyone except me and the kids. People need to get out once in a while and vent to people that are...not their husband or wife."

"Oh, yeah? Is that what you do?"

"Sometimes."

"Who are you venting to, Ron?"

I stay silent.

"I have friends," Kate continues. "Trust me, I vent to Kay at work all the time. It still doesn't change the fact that you, my husband, are not fulfilling my needs as your wife. God, forget what I said downstairs. I've changed my mind. I *should* have an affair, just so I can remember what it feels like to be with a man who thinks I'm interesting and wants to talk to me."

"Nice," I say, hurt, and unsure how to properly vocalize my emotions. I think of Courtney again and realize that she is somehow adding fuel to my fire, because in the back of my mind, I'm aware that I have someone else outside waiting for me. A backup plan. "I'm not like you, Kate. Christ, I feel like you'd be happier married to a woman. I know you don't swing that way, but hell, at this point the pros might outweigh the cons."

"Wow," says Kate.

"Is that what you need? Because I'm beginning to think that's the only way you're ever going to feel fulfilled in a relationship."

"You actually just said that." She shakes her head in disbelief. "I feel like I don't even know who you are anymore."

"Yeah, well, that makes two of us," I say.

"You don't know who you are anymore either?"

"Funny," I say, unamused and quickly losing control. "And to think I was convinced that you actually wanted to have sex with me tonight. God forbid. I don't know when that turned into such a crime."

"It's not," she says. "But you have to earn it first."

"And that, my dear, is exactly why you feel so alone."

She glares at me. Her chest rises and falls, fast and heavy.

"So…" I say. "Have we done enough talking for one night? Or is there more you wish to discuss?"

She shifts her body a few inches away from mine, creating more space for our angry words to fill. "Let me ask you this, Ron: where do you see yourself in five years? Ten years? Am I even there with you?"

"Of course you are, why wouldn't you be?"

"Gee, I don't know. Maybe because our marriage is falling apart, and as far as I can tell, you have no interest in fixing it. Or perhaps you've just been too busy to notice."

"Of course I want to fix it. It's all I think about. Why do you keep talking to me like I'm one of the kids? I'm your husband, for Christ's sake!" My lips tremble.

She reaches through the buzzing swarm of angry words and takes my face in her hands. "Look me in the eye and tell me that, without a doubt, when you imagine your future, years from now, you see me there next to you."

I breathe in and out slowly, trying to keep it together.

"Honestly," she says.

"I can't do that."

She nods. Her lips press firmly together.

"But that doesn't mean I don't want you to be. I'm just being realistic, is all. Especially given our current situation. There are no guarantees."

"Whatever you say."

"Am I there with you?" I ask.

"You were. But right now, I'm not so sure."

"Is that so?"

"Yeah. And don't pretend like you don't have one foot out the door already, Ron. I'm not stupid. Hell, I'm sure you would have left me already if not for the girls. They're the ones that make you happy, not me."

I'm losing her. I'm losing her right now, and the worst part is, I don't care. Not right now, at least. I'm too exhausted from this endless routine to care.

"I can't win with you. No matter what I say or do, it's always wrong. And it's always a fight—"

"Bullshit! That's a bullshit cop-out and you know it."

"It's not bullshit! It's been like this for months, and you know it. Sooner or later, I'm bound to reach a point where I ask myself, why bother?"

"Why bother?" she repeats.

"You know what I mean."

She shakes her head. "I don't think you even love me anymore. You still haven't asked me how my appointment went this morning. That speaks louder than any of your words. So, do what you want, Ron. This obviously isn't working out. You're free to leave. Don't let me stand in your way."

"Kate…"

"I mean, we made it twelve whole years. That's more than most. We should be proud of ourselves."

"Kate, don't…"

"It's no problem, Ron. If I'm more than you can handle, then good riddance. If you want to leave and start over with someone younger and prettier than me, then be my guest. Do what you need to do."

"Fine," I say. "Perhaps that would be best."

We stare at each other until the silence starts to drown, no longer able to hold its breath.

"So, what now?" I ask.

"You tell me. I just laid it all out for you. I can't possibly make it any easier for you."

We stare at each other some more.

She lets out a tiny sigh and holds my face in her hands once again. "Do you still love me?" she asks. "Yes or no." Tears run down her cheeks. "And by love, I don't mean the attachment or dedication you feel toward me, because I've always been here with you, and it's all you know. Or because I'm the mother of your children. But because I'm still the one who makes your life worth living. Because there's no one else you'd rather wake up next to. Because you still get excited when you think of our future together. And most of all, because you can't imagine life with anyone else, no matter how bad things get. No matter who else you run into or meet along the way. Because this is our journey, Ron. Ours. Nobody else's."

I close my eyes for a moment, trying to hold back my own tears.

"Be honest," she says. "Not just with me, but with yourself."

I hesitate, unsure if honesty is the best choice in moments such as these, or if I even know what my honest feelings are anymore. How much of it has become clouded by outside influences and unnecessary stress?

"Yes, I love you."

"Are you sure? Because I know from the bottom of my heart that I love you."

"I'm sure," I say. "I'm just not sure love is enough."

She nods. "I understand. I suppose it's time to try something else. Put some space between us. I mean, let's be honest, this is just too much."

"I know. I'm sorry, Kate." My voice quivers. "I never meant for things to get like this."

She nods, teary-eyed. "Yeah, me neither. Sucks to be us, I guess." She lies down on her side with her back facing me. "Good night, Ron." She sniffles.

I slump back against the headboard, my frustration quickly getting the better of my judgment. "I don't remember this being so difficult before. Why did we let so much get in the way? Did you ever stop to think that maybe if you didn't make it so much work, I might be less frustrated and would have an easier time opening up to you? You're not the easiest person to talk to, you know?"

She turns toward me, scowling.

"Think about it," I say. "If you didn't put so much energy into giving me attitude, I might actually have the energy to talk to you, instead of wasting it arguing about every little thing." There's no way for these words to not sound mean and harsh coming out of my mouth. But I wish to God there was because I'm not trying to be mean. I'm just being honest.

She flares her nostrils. Then she sits up, straightens her shirt out, and wipes away a tear. "You're an asshole. Thanks for shifting all the blame onto me. I can't talk about this anymore tonight. I need space to think. I suggest you do the same and get back to me when you've made a firm decision about what it is you do or don't want to do with your life. If you're still not one hundred percent sure you want to be with me, then I want a divorce, and you need to find someplace else to live. It's as simple as that. Now, get away from me."

My heart plunges against my chest like it's moving sideways, scraping against my ribcage. We can't end things this way. Already, I'm mournful. I want to travel back in time to when I still made Kate happy.

The girls' faces flash in my mind, and a lump forms in my throat. "What about the girls?"

"I said I can't talk about this anymore tonight."

"Kate..."

She sits up in bed, breathing heavy like she's possessed. "Do I look like I'm joking, Ron? Get away from me *right now*, before I freak the fuck out."

"Kate, I'm sorry. You're right about everything. I've been awful. I'll do better, I promise."

"Stop saying that!" She grabs her lion-shaped piggy bank off the bedside table and throws it at me. I duck, and it shatters against the wall with a devastatingly loud crash. Coins, along with a thousand tiny pieces of porcelain, fall to the floor. The mess is immense and everywhere. I've never seen her this worked up before. Thank God the girls aren't here.

"What the hell is wrong with you? Are you nuts?"

"Get out!" she yells.

"Where do you want me to go?"

"I don't care. Anywhere but here. Go sleep in the goddamn guest room." She points to the door.

"I'm not sleeping in the goddamn guest room," I say. For a moment, the very air in the room appears to have heat waves.

Her eyes widen with rage, and I turn away from her. I know that if I don't leave right now, then she'll find something else to throw at me.

"Fine," I say.

She flips back over on her side, away from me, and turns out the light. I turn the bathroom light on and take a moment to try and pick the broken pieces up off the floor. It takes two hands to get it all. The rest will need to be vacuumed. I'll worry about the coins later.

I stand inside the bathroom doorway, blinded by the light. I squeeze the broken glass inside my fists until it hurts.

"Happy anniversary," Kate says behind me.

CHAPTER TEN

THE GUEST BED

I get in the shower, hoping that the warmth and familiarity will help me unwind, but instead, my frustration consumes me. I barely feel the water on my skin. The feeling digs in deeper. There's nothing to console me. After I get out, I throw on a fresh pair of boxers and a t-shirt and glance at Kate. She's still on her side with her back to me. Her breathing is slow and regulated, giving off the slightest hint of a light snore; the tiny buzz emanating from her mouth. She's asleep.

Downstairs in the guest room, I throw myself on the bed with clenched fists, punching the pillows several times. Once I've tired myself out, I roll over and stare up at the window on the wall behind me, watching the rain pound against the glass.

Damn you, Kate. If that's how you want it, fine. I'm out. I'm better off without you. I'll find someone else. Someone who can talk to me without making me feel stupid.

Wait.

I have that, already. Outside, in my car. Courtney. I might as well bring her in here with me. At least she enjoys my company.

A shadow moves across the room. I catch it in the corner of my eye, and my mind fights against my sight to convince me that it was nothing. I glance around the darkness. I've never liked this room. It gives me the creeps. There's something self-righteous about it. It's too perfect. Not a speck of dust. Everything in its rightful place. The bed is always made, never a single crease. It's smug, and as cynical as the woman who cleans it.

I reach toward the bedside table for my phone to check the time and discover I never brought it with me. It must be upstairs in the bedroom somewhere.

Lightning flashes outside the window and lights up the room. Thunder roars. It's getting cold. I picture Courtney in my car, shivering.

That's it. I'm going outside to get her. Or at least to bring her a blanket. One or the other, I haven't decided yet.

I grab one of the blankets from the guest bedroom, taking great pleasure in crumpling it up and shoving it under my arm. I head out to the car where I find Courtney, asleep but shivering. The sight of her puts me at ease. Her aroma is everywhere. She's wrapped herself up tightly in my jacket, but it isn't doing much to keep her warm.

I shake her shoulder. "Hey, Courtney. Wake up."

"Hey," she says, opening her eyes. Her voice is scratchy, her lips dark and quivering.

"How was dinner?"

"It was perfect, thank you."

"I brought you a blanket."

"Oh my God, thank you so much. I'm freezing."

"I thought you might be."

She slides my jacket off her body, and it lands on the floor next to her. She wraps the blanket around her as tight as she can.

I can't make her stay out here in the cold like an animal. She's freezing, and one blanket won't change that. She shouldn't be punished for my mistakes. It's not her fault I lied to Kate.

"Come on," I say. "You're coming inside with me."

"What about your wife?"

"Don't worry, I'll close the door. She'll never know you're there. In the morning, we'll get up, have breakfast together, and then I'll take you back to your car."

"Sounds perfect."

I take her hand and help her out of the car, then we run through the rain and into the house. She follows me down the hallway, holding onto my arm the whole time. By the time she lies down on the guest bed, she's nearly asleep again. As I go to pull the blanket up over her, I notice that her feet are bare. She must have taken her heels off in the car.

I kneel next to Courtney. She smiles sleepily with one hand resting on my arm, caressing my skin with the tips of her fingers. Her eyes glow in the darkness, like a wolf watching its prey from the safety of the trees, its true shape hidden. The invitation is there, but I can't accept it.

"Goodnight, Courtney."

"Goodnight, Ron."

Her teeth chatter. I place my hand against her cheek. Her skin feels like ice. I go to the closet to grab an extra blanket, perfectly folded and clean. I return to the bed and spread it over her, but as I'm pulling away, she grabs my wrist.

"Will you lie with me?" she asks. "Just for a few minutes? I'm so cold."

A few minutes won't hurt. It's not like I have a lot of options. It's this or the couch.

I crawl into the bed with her. She presses herself against my side, wrapping her arm around me and resting her head on my shoulder. My cheek is pressed against her cold forehead, and I hold her tight, trying to warm her up. Her sweet scent consumes me. It stirs my senses. It doesn't take long for her body to warm in my arms.

Who am I right now? I don't even recognize myself.

Am I really in bed with another woman? With Kate upstairs, directly above us, unaware? It's so surreal. This may be the strangest day of my life.

Courtney's breath flows slowly and evenly. I rub her back. She twitches and tightens her grip. Her blouse is untucked. I move my hand underneath it and caress her skin with my fingers, moving up and down along the sides of her spine. She makes a quick, pleasant humming noise as I struggle beneath the weight of my own desires. The touch of her bare skin makes my body tingle, like the storm outside is charging my fingers with electricity.

Outside, lightning strikes again. Less than a second later, thunder echoes through my silent house, causing Courtney to jolt in my arms. I stare up at the ceiling, where Kate lies directly above us, and suddenly I don't feel good about any of this. My stomach rumbles with hunger and anxiety. My eyelids are getting heavy, but I don't want to fall asleep here. Must...get...up...

***

I'm sitting on the floor of an empty bottle surrounded by thick opaque walls. When I pound my fists against the glass and scream for help, my cries echo back louder and louder. Kate's face appears above me, through the bottleneck. It's enormous. She blocks the opening above my head as she peers down curiously at me. I try to speak—beg for help—but she doesn't hear me. She's too busy talking over me. Her voice comes blasting out like a freight train straight down into the bottle. It ruptures my eardrums and jars my body. I hunker down, helpless, unable to communicate, unable to even make out her words through the pain they're causing.

***

I wake, wondering how long I've been asleep. It's still dark outside, thank God. This room could use a clock. Courtney is sound asleep in my arms. Her arm is curled inside my shirt, her hand resting on my bare chest. She feels foreign in my arms.

I try to get up, hoping to sneak out of the room, but Courtney lets out another tiny moan, and I freeze as she spreads her fingers around on my chest. I try to move again, but she pulls her hand out from under my shirt and moves it up to the side of my face. She shifts closer, her entire body now pressed against mine, her leg coiled across my midsection.

Her lips are on my neck, planting small, soft kisses. Then my cheek. Then my lips: once, twice, three times. Each peck is filled with a longing that tugs at my chest and holds me immobile. When I don't pull away, she presses her lips to mine once more, letting them linger. My lips soften under hers for one brief, yearning moment.

134 · LUKE P. NARLEE

She climbs on top of me, kissing me more, moving her tongue around inside my mouth. I know it's wrong, but I can't bring myself to stop her. Not yet. I need this comfort, even if I don't deserve it.

Soon, I tell myself as I bring my hand higher, underneath the back of her shirt, feeling around her shoulder blades. Small tingles and sparks of pleasure flash and spread through my body. I think of this morning when I touched Kate's back the same way.

We need to stop. We're veering too close to the point of no return.

She lifts her shirt up over her head and drops it down on the floor. I rest my hands on her legs for a moment, then out of sheer guilt, I drop them to my sides, holding my palms flat against the mattress. I do my best to keep them pinned down, but she grabs my right wrist and holds my hand up against one of her breasts, over her bra.

This is too much. I can't let this happen.

She moves her other hand down toward my waist and tugs on my waistband, and I use every bit of willpower I can summon to slip out from under her and leave the bed.

"What's wrong?" she asks. "Where are you going?"

"I can't do this," I say. "I have to go."

"Already?"

I don't have it in me to convince her that this is wrong, for more reasons than I can name. Instead, I flee to the guest bathroom and lock the door. After taking a minute to collect myself, I sit on the toilet and hold my face in my hands, hoping to God that she'll go back to sleep.

I hear odd shuffling-like movements outside the door. I sense her standing there. She knocks twice against the door, slow and steady. Chills run up my back. An image of her friend's decrepit house flashes through my mind.

"I'll be out in a minute..." I say.

A few seconds later the bed squeaks a couple times like she's crawling back into it. I wait five minutes and then leave the bathroom. It's too dark to see anything. I take a couple of steps and discover a soft article of clothing under my foot. I bend and pick it up, but can't make out what it is. I press it to my nose. Courtney seeps through my nostrils and pulls my eyelids shut, luring me into another dimension for a moment. I drop it back on the floor and wait for my eyes to adjust.

Where is she?

I whisper into the darkness. "Courtney?"

Someone whispers back, a few feet away, only it's indecipherable. I get the strange sense that Kate is in the room with me. Hiding in the corner, watching me. Putting the pieces together. I feel someone's breath on my neck. My body jolts and I wave my arm around, but there's nobody there.

A floorboard creaks somewhere in the room. My body is stiff with fear.

"Courtney?"

Someone whispers my name. It must be Courtney.

Lightning flashes, and I catch a glimpse of the empty, disturbed bed, covered with ruffled sheets and blankets. I wait for the next flash. A floorboard creaks again, closer to me this time.

The lightning flashes and illuminates the entire bed. Courtney is in it, lying naked on her side; her body lies twisted in some abstract fetal position, curled like a snake. There's a teddy bear on the pillow next to her. It was Lilly's from when she was two. She used to take it with her everywhere. It's been in the attic for years.

How the hell did it wind up in here? It's a sign. Even from forty miles away, one of my daughters found a way to reach out, begging me to do the right thing and leave this room as soon as possible. To keep our family together. Lightning flashes again, and thunder rumbles. Courtney's head is tucked down toward her chest, so I can't tell if she's awake or not.

I'm getting out of here.

I tiptoe out the door and shut it firmly behind me, fighting the irrational urge to bar it somehow. I pad up the stairs to my real bedroom—hoping like hell that Courtney won't follow me. I feel a slight sting enter the bottom of my foot as I pass through the room. Before crawling back into bed with Kate, I lift my foot and feel for glass or blood but find nothing.

Lying there in the darkness, I can see the outline of a body. It could be anyone. I'm barely able to make out the long strands of her hair, which from this angle look more like giant spider legs.

My foot still hurts. I rub my foot against my leg to try and wipe away the sting, but it only makes it worse.

The thunder and lightning seem to have stopped, but the rain is coming down harder than ever, pounding against the roof of the house like a million tiny nails.

I can't believe I never asked how her appointment went. I'm such an idiot. For all I know, she's on some strange new medication. That could be why she was acting so different earlier. I doubt it, though. I don't think meds work that fast. I should have asked her. Instead, I forgot again.

She was right… Everything she said this morning was true. She deserves better.

My eyes fill with tears as I press my fingers to her back, feeling alone. Is this how I make her feel?

I'm so sorry, Kate. I miss you.

What am I doing with my life? Have I screwed it up beyond repair, or do I still have time to fix it?

I'll make time.

First, I need to deal with Courtney and get her out of my house and my life. I'll wake her up in the morning, we'll eat breakfast, and I'll send her on her way. No more temptations. No more fantasies.

As I drift back to sleep with one hand on Kate's back, I'm haunted by the image of Courtney lying below me on the guest bed, naked and alone. Her body twisting into weird, serpent-like positions. It gnaws at my mind. Bites down on it. I envision the guest room as a giant casket, buried beneath me, deep in the ground. Then, the echo of Courtney's voice in the distance, calling out, begging for help. Or is it Kate's voice?

Part 2

"A successful marriage requires falling in love many times, always with the same person."

— MIGNON MCLAUGHLIN

CHAPTER ELEVEN

FRESH START

The room is bright and alive with sunshine. Outside the window, the sky is blue. Kate's body rests against my back, and her arm is wrapped around my waist underneath the blankets. Could she have forgiven me already? I reach under and caress her arm with my hand. The touch of her skin brings a smile to my face.

I study the light pouring in through the window, spreading itself along the floor. It's a beautiful day, and I'm in my wife's loving arms on the morning of our anniversary. It doesn't get any better. Maybe I'll leave work early today and take her out to dinner to celebrate. Some place quiet and romantic. It'll be wonderful.

This feels good. Things are looking up.

I check the clock. 7:03 a.m. She should have left already.

Today is our anniversary.

The realization brings me both joy and regret. I still don't have a gift for her, even though I implied otherwise. The day will be ruined if she figures out that I lied. She won't though. I just need to have a gift by tonight. Everything will be fine.

Maybe if I hadn't spent the entire evening focused on Courtney...

Courtney!

Panic shoots through me like a shotgun blast. How could I
forget?

I check the clock again. This isn't good. Why is Kate here?
Did she take the day off from work? No, she doesn't do that
without good reason. Follow-up medical appointment? Too
soon. To celebrate our anniversary? Possible, but doubtful.
What am I going to do? Of all the days to stay home...
Courtney will be up any minute, if she isn't already, expecting
Kate to be at work. What if she comes up here to wake me?
They'll see each other. It'll be a disaster. If that happens, Kate
will leave me for sure.

I slip out of bed and run downstairs and peek into the guest
room. The bed is empty and perfectly made as if no one ever
set foot in there last night. Maybe it was all a bad dream. I laugh
to myself and breathe a sigh of relief. She must have left. But
how? She doesn't have her car here. Taxi? Or...is she lurking
somewhere in the house? My anxiety returns, and I remember
the flashes of lightning from last night, the way they illumi-
nated her strangely contorted body. I search every room
downstairs but don't find her anywhere. She must have left.
Thank God.

I go back upstairs to the bedroom, relaxed and content once
again. Ready to have a great day. I get back into my bed with
my lovely wife, who is now buried under the covers. I reach
under and find her arm again.

"Hon, wake up. You're late for work."

"Mm..." she moans.

"Come on, beautiful. It's time to get up."

"No way, I'm staying home today." Her voice knocks the wind right out of me, and suddenly I'm paralyzed. That isn't Kate's voice. "You should call in sick like I did, so we can spend the day in bed together," Courtney continues.

I rip the covers off her and stare at Courtney in disbelief. She's there, lying in my bed, wearing pink and white striped pajamas that I've never laid eyes on before.

"Hey! Be nice," she says, grabbing the blankets and pulling them back over her.

"Courtney?"

She peeks her head out. "Yeah?"

I catch my breath. It was Kate who left the house already. I should have known she wouldn't lie so close to me after the fight we had.

All the enthusiasm deflates from my body as I collapse against the headboard. "You gave me a heart attack."

"And how on earth did I do that?" she asks, her voice still rough and scratchy from sleep.

"By being here in bed with me, obviously. I thought you were Kate."

She rubs her eyes a few times and looks at me, confused. "Who the hell is Kate?"

"Funny," I say. "How long have you been in here?"

"Um… Since I fell asleep last night."

"Huh?"

"Oh! By the way…" She sits up, excited. "Happy anniversary!" She kisses me. I stare at her, confused. "What's wrong?" she asks.

"Courtney."

"Yeah?" she blinks, her eyes full of innocence.

"I don't want to do this with you."

"Oh… Okay, well, we could exchange gifts later, if you prefer."

"No, I mean, you shouldn't be here like this. It's a mistake. This whole thing has been a giant mistake."

"What do you mean?" Her face droops with such sadness and confusion, I don't know whether to feel anger or pity.

"I mean we can't lie in bed together. It's not right. Come on, it's time to go. I need to get to work."

She grunts and flops on the bed dramatically. "Ugh! You're so lame."

"Lame? Are you insane? You're lucky to be alive right now. If Kate saw you here in this bed, God only knows what she might have done."

Courtney sits up. "Okay, seriously, who's Kate, and what are you talking about?"

"Don't play stupid. You already know she's my wife."

"Your wife?"

"Yes, my wife."

Her mouth forms a small smirk, then she laughs.

"What's so funny?" I ask.

"Oh, I don't know. It's just that, last time I checked, *I* was your wife."

I chuckle. "You're obviously insane."

"Are you even awake right now?" She waves her hand in front of my face. Her smile fades a bit. "Aw, baby. I know what it is." She runs her fingers through my hair. "You were dreaming, that's all."

"Say what?"

"That's why you're so confused. You're having one of your episodes. It's part of your DRC issue that you have periodically. I swear you have narcolepsy or something."

"DRC?"

"Yeah. Dream reality confusion. It's when you dream at night and become so involved in the dream that you wake up confused by reality. You get the two backwards in your mind. You really don't remember any of this?"

"No, because that's not a real thing."

"Uh, yeah, it is a real thing. Look it up if you don't believe me."

I shake my head. "Regardless, I'm not confused about anything, except for why you're here in bed with me, and my wife, Kate, isn't."

"Well, sometimes these spells are more confusing for you than other times. This looks like a bad one."

"Courtney."

"Yeah."

"I didn't just dream my entire life prior to this morning."

"Well, no. I didn't suggest that you had."

I feel my body start to tremble. A light sweat breaks out on my forehead.

"Ron, it's okay. I'm here with you." She holds my hand. "I promise, everything will feel normal again in just a few minutes. Just give it some time."

This can't be real. This is not a thing. I didn't just imagine Kate and all we've been going through. That's ridiculous.

I pull my hand away. "Where's Kate?" I ask again.

Courtney shrugs. "Couldn't tell you."

"I didn't invent her with my mind."

"Perhaps not. Honestly, she's probably someone you know."

"Someone I know…" I repeat.

"Yeah. Like a co-worker or something. Or maybe someone you met briefly on the train. But I promise she's not your wife."

I think back to when I woke up on the train yesterday and found Courtney there next to me.

"I met *you* on a train," I say. "Yesterday."

"Hmm, no, you met me in a bookstore fourteen years ago."

I massage my forehead, trying to control myself from going into a full throttle panic attack.

Her eyes roam my face, full of concern. "Aww, baby, you're really struggling this time. It's okay; come here." She pulls me into her and wraps her arms around me, holding me tight. She strokes the hair on the back of my head with her hand. "Just give it a few minutes, okay? You'll be fine, I promise."

Her sympathy is refreshing. But this is still jacked up. I have to do something. I can't just sit here and let this happen.

I pull away from her. "All right, joke's over. You've had your fun. Come on." I snap my fingers.

She pushes her lips together like she's trying not to laugh.

"I'm not kidding. Get up and get dressed. I'm done playing games with you."

"Ron, I need you to calm down and trust me on this one. This *will* pass. Right now I just want you to pick up the phone and call out of work so that you can stay home with me. It's our anniversary, and I want to celebrate it with you."

"Okay… Here's the deal. We're done talking about this."

"All right."

"I'm not crazy," I say.

"I know that."

"Good. I'm glad you know that. Now do you want to know what I know? I know I don't suffer from DRM or whatever the hell you said earlier." Courtney sighs and crosses her arms. "I also know I didn't dream up my life. And I know for certain that I'm not married to you. I'm married to Kate. She's alive and well. I just have to figure out where she is. So that's what I'm going to do."

"Ron..."

"Please stop messing with my head. You can miss as many days of work as you want, but you can't do it here. Now, get dressed so I can take you back to your creepy friend's house, or the parking garage, or wherever it is you need to go."

She throws her hands in the air. "What are you talking about?"

"I'm talking about you leaving, so you can continue on with your own life, instead of trying to take over mine."

"Even if I were to go to work today, you'd still have to drive me. My car will be in the shop until Friday, you know that."

"In the shop my ass. It's sitting right where we left it last night; inside the train station parking garage."

"Last night? What? Ron... You're starting to make me nervous. Can we please just try to have a good day together? God, why does this have to happen today, of all days?"

I shake my head. "I never should have brought you here. I don't know what I was thinking."

She rolls her eyes. "Oh my God, you're acting so weird."

"How do you expect me to act when you jump into bed with me and pretend to be Kate?"

"I'm not pretending to be anyone! I'm your wife. We've been married for twelve years."

I breathe in deeply through my nose and run my hands through my hair. "Courtney, this isn't complicated. Get out of my house."

She shakes her head back and forth, slowly. "No way. I'm not going anywhere."

"Fine. Have it your way. I'm calling the police."

She laughs. "And telling them what, Ron? My wife is home with me and won't leave, please arrest her?"

"I'll tell them there's a crazy woman in my house who's convinced she's my wife and refuses to leave."

She tilts her head and squints as if viewing the situation in a new light. "You're serious, aren't you? You really want me to leave?"

"Yes. That's exactly what I want. I think I've made that pretty clear."

"And you want me to go where?"

"Anywhere. Anywhere but here. Back to wherever you came from. Parking garage. New apartment. Storage facility. Hole in the ground. I don't care."

"Nice, Ron. Really nice. You know what? I'm trying really hard to not take this personally, but you're making it really difficult."

I get out of bed and search through my closet for a shirt.

She slides to the edge of the bed and brushes a string of hair out of her eyes. "I have to stay strong for you. I know that. That's why I'm just going to carry on like normal and wait for this to pass."

I stand in front of the mirror and button my shirt. "Look, Courtney. You're a sweet girl. I enjoyed hanging out and chatting with you for a night, but it's over now. I'm married. I don't want to hang out with you anymore. I'm sorry if things didn't work out the way you wanted." There, that ought to settle it once and for all.

Courtney starts laughing hysterically.

I shake my head. "Jesus Christ. You really are a sad, lonely person, aren't you?"

She stops laughing and her face turns serious. For the first time this morning, it appears that I've hurt her feelings.

"Don't look at me like that," I say. "Twenty minutes, Courtney. You have twenty minutes. If you're not ready to go by then, I'm calling the police. Use the shower if you need to."

"Gee, thanks," she says. "I'm overwhelmed by your kindness."

I go to grab my phone off the charger, but my phone isn't there. I search the room: on top of the bed, under it, and in the pants I wore yesterday. "Goddamn it!" I yell. "Courtney, do you know where I left my phone?"

She scowls so hard, wrinkles form along her forehead, expressing both anger and hurt. "No. Why don't you go back to sleep and ask your fantasy wife, Kate? Maybe she can tell you."

I leave the bedroom and walk downstairs, trying to remember where I saw it last. Maybe I brought it to the guest room last night. I peek my head inside the room. It still looks the same. Spotless. A little too spotless. No cell phone, either. I step into the guest bathroom and look for signs of wetness in the sink from when I washed my face off a few hours earlier.

Nothing.

I close the door and stand in the hallway to think.

Last time I used it was last night, in the car with Courtney. I called Kate to let her know I'd be late. What the hell happened to it after that?

I need to call Kate at work. That's what I'll do. I'll use the home phone. I'll tell her I woke up and found a strange woman in our bed, and she won't leave. Kate will know how to handle this. She's resourceful like that.

I grab the phone off the kitchen wall and speed-dial Kate's cell phone. *Sorry to do this to you, Courtney, but you've left me no choice.*

I wait for her to pick up, but it's not happening. No voicemail either. I hang up and dial Kate's office instead. The receptionist answers. "Grant and Williams, how may I direct your call?"

"Hey, Penelope, it's Ron Cordova. May I speak to my wife, please?"

"Hey, Ron. Courtney's not here today."

"Excuse me?"

"She called out sick earlier this morning."

"I don't believe this," I say.

"Said she had a sore throat or something."

"Why did you say Courtney and not Kate? My wife's name is Kate."

"Okay, I'm confused. This is Ron Cordova, right?"

"Yes."

"And you're looking for your wife, Courtney Cordova?"

"No, you must have another Cordova in the office. I want to talk to Kate. Will you please connect me to her?"

After a brief pause, she says, "I'm sorry, Ron. I'm not sure what to tell you. Nobody named Kate works here in this office."

I do my best to stay calm.

"Ron?"

"Thanks for your help." I hang up the phone, nauseous.

Where the hell is Kate? I want my wife back.

I run back upstairs. There's water running in the shower. I go into the bathroom and rip the shower curtain open. Courtney jumps and places her hand over her heart, her hair full of shampoo. "Jesus... You scared the hell out of me." She lifts her arms and massages the shampoo in her hair. "You got me good that time. Don't worry, I'll get you back. Right when you least expect it." The sight of her naked body is jarring, and further cements my certainty that she's not my wife. "What? Is my time up already?" She smirks.

I open my mouth to speak, but nothing comes out.

Her smile fades. "Okay, now you're just being creepy." She pulls the shower curtain closed.

I pull it open. "Where is Kate?"

"Christ, not this again." She pulls it back.

I pull it open. "Why are you doing this? Is this like a *Fatal Attraction* thing? What's next? Are you going to threaten me and my family if I don't choose you?"

Courtney pours a dab of some fancy, expensive-looking body soap into a washcloth and rubs it against her arms. Kate would never buy something like that, so it must be Courtney's. What if she killed Kate and buried her in the backyard somewhere?

"Look, Ron," she says, "I don't know what's going on with you today, or why you're having such a hard time, but I'm seriously starting to worry. Are you having a mid-life crisis?" She eyes me up and starts to smile. "Why don't you get in here with me? I know what will make you feel better."

"I don't think so."

"Fine. Go to work then. See if I care. I wouldn't mind some time alone for once, anyway. When you get home tonight, we can try again. Fresh start."

"Fresh start..."

"I was hoping we could stay home together at least once this week before the girls come back. And I figured our anniversary was the ideal choice, but I can see that's not going to happen."

The girls. It didn't even cross my mind how this might affect them. *Sorry, kids, but your mom went through a few changes while you were away. Now she looks and acts like a different person, but I promise she's still your mother, so no worries. Okay?*

"Don't mention my kids," I say.

She tilts her head. "Now you're just being mean."

"Courtney, I don't want a fresh start with you. Just tell me where Kate is."

She turns the water off. "Ron, I swear, if I hear that name come out of your mouth one more time, I'm going to explode."

Frustration boils up through my entire body, threatening to shoot out through the top of my head. I point my finger at her. "Courtney, I'm not telling you again. Get dressed and get out of my house now!"

She presses her now trembling palms against her temples. "Ron, please stop yelling at me. You're scaring me."

She's visibly upset. And still naked...

"Okay, I'm sorry. I'll stop yelling."

She lowers her hands, wiping a tear from her cheek.

I grab a clean towel off the rack and hand it to her. "You do need to leave, though."

She moves her glistening eyes all around my face, worried and defensive.

A lump grows in my throat again and suddenly I'm fighting back tears myself.

She frowns sympathetically, as if finally realizing how much I'm struggling. She tries to hold my chin in her soapy hand, but I resist.

"I'm calling your doctor as soon as you leave for work."

"No, you're not."

"Yes. I am. I have to do something. I can't just sit back and watch you deteriorate. He needs to know about this. Maybe he can help."

"The kids will be back in a few days," I say under my breath. "What am I going to do? They'll be so confused."

Courtney reaches out to touch me with shaky hands, but changes her mind and pulls back. "Ron, sweetie, what's happening to you? Tell me what's running through your mind right now. I want to help."

I shake my head. "My God, what have I done?" I lean against the wall and slide to the floor. "Please," my voice quivers. "I just want my wife back. What did you do with her?"

"Jesus, maybe you have a brain tumor." She places her hand against her head. "Forget the sleeping problem. What if it's cancer? Or worse?"

She steps out of the shower. Suds roll down her legs onto the floor. She crouches in front of me. "I know you've been under a lot of stress, and God knows I've been difficult to deal with lately. But don't worry about any of that... I forgive you for everything. Now, let's build on this so we can get our lives back on track and carry on like the amazing couple I know we are." I look at her. "Can we do that, please?"

"I need to get out of here." I stand. She does the same. Her eyes are sad. I place my hands on her shoulders. "Please be gone when I get home tonight. That's all I ask." I turn to walk away, then hesitate. "Oh, and, I swear, if you did anything to Kate... If you're responsible for her disappearance... I *will* find you. And I *will* make sure you suffer the consequences."

Little sobs and sniffles echo from the bathroom as I finish getting ready.

I go to leave the room, but when I turn to the door, she's standing in my way with bloodshot eyes, her towel wrapped around her.

"I'm sorry, Courtney. I don't mean to hurt you, but you don't belong here."

I walk around her and go downstairs. On my way down, I hear her yell, "This is bullshit, Ron! You can't treat me like this. It's not right. I didn't do anything to your precious Kate!"

I grab my keys and observe the wall in front of me. There's an unfamiliar, abstract painting on it, hanging right where our family portrait used to be.

"Where's the photo that used to be here?" I yell. Instead of waiting for a response, I start to search the house for photos of Kate. But wherever I look, all I find are photos of the girls. She does always say we don't take enough pictures of her. Is that the only family portrait we have in this house? There's got to be another way to know for sure. If only I could find my damn phone.

In the kitchen, I spot a small photo of Courtney on the fridge. It's wedged between photos of the kids. In the picture, she is leaning against a brick wall, posing. Smiling. I pick it up and look at it. I've never seen this picture before.

I have a framed picture of Kate on my desk at work.

If I'm not crazy, and if there's a rational explanation for this, then that photo of Kate will still be there. Courtney could have placed her picture on the fridge last night. She could have removed the portrait from the wall. But she couldn't have moved the picture in my office. She doesn't even know where I work. Or does she? Even if she does, there's no way she could have gone in there and switched them between the time I left last night and this morning. She's been with me the whole time.

The photo slips out of my fingers and falls to the floor. When it lands, it slides underneath the fridge.

I head back to the hallway.

Courtney appears at the top of the stairs. "Ron, please don't leave me like this. I'm begging you. Stay here with me. We'll figure this out together."

"I'm going to work. I guess you can stay here for now. I need to check a couple of things, but I'll call you later with an update. If I find what I'm looking for, I'll let you know, and you'll need to leave immediately. If I don't, then I'll come home to you tonight, and we'll try to figure this out together. That's the most I can offer you right now."

She sniffs back tears and nods. "Okay."

"Did you move the picture off the wall by the coat hangers? The family portrait?"

She sniffs again. "No. We don't have any family portraits. I keep asking you if we can have one made, but..."

I walk to the front door.

"Ron?"

"What?"

"What can I do to prove I'm your wife? There must be something."

I walk to the bottom of the stairs. "What month did we get married?" I ask her.

"July."

"Where did we go for our honeymoon?"

"Jamaica."

"What's my favorite sport?"

"Basketball."

I shake my head in disbelief. "This doesn't make any sense."

"I'm your wife, Ron. Why don't you believe me?" There's real desperation in her voice now. She runs down the stairs and holds my face. "Ron, look at me. Everything's going to be fine. You just have to give it more time, and you'll see that everything is exactly how it's supposed to be."

It won't be fine. Not if I don't find Kate.

"Stay home. Be with me. You shouldn't go anywhere in this condition."

"I have to go, Courtney."

"Tell me what's wrong. I can't help you if you don't open up to me. Let me call your doctor for you."

I shake my head.

"Please. Whatever you need. You need to see someone. I'm worried about you." Her voice is shaking, and fresh tears gather in her eyes.

How am I supposed to accept this change and continue living as if nothing happened? Is this what it means to start over? Because, if so, I don't want any part of it.

"I have to go," I say again. "I can't discuss this with you anymore."

"Wait. Ron—"

"No." I pry her hands off of me. "I need to go to my office. If the picture is different, then I'll be back. I promise." I grab my bag and walk out the door.

Right before the door closes, I hear her yell: "And what if it isn't?"

CHAPTER TWELVE

BACK AT THE OFFICE

I walk up to my car and see that the door is still dented. I scratch my head and glance at the house. It seems like it should be a good thing that the dent is still there, but I have no idea what it means in terms of Kate being gone.

Driving to the train station, my mind feels numb, despite a million thoughts stampeding through it. I forgot to brush my hair. I don't think I even showered. What if I'm crazy? I need to call my kids.

Heading down the main road, it occurs to me that the jogger isn't appearing in her usual spot. No sign of her at all.

No smile. No wave.

The rest of my morning commute is disconcertingly normal, only I don't care who sits next to me on the train. I don't even care where I sit. The front bumper of the train will work just fine.

When I get to my office, I rush to my desk and grab the framed photo that rests there. My heart sinks as my eyes meet Courtney's. What little energy I had left drains from my body.

If Courtney's my wife, then there's no rational explanation besides a severe mental collapse on my part. No, I refuse to accept that. I have to believe that Kate still exists somewhere. She must.

My supervisor, Tom, a tall, burly man with glasses and a receding hairline, steps into my office. He's scribbling away at his ever-present clipboard. My mind barely registers his entrance.

"Good morning, Ron. How are things?"

"Awful."

"Sorry to hear that," he says, still writing. "Don't forget we have a two o'clock meeting."

"Okay," I say.

Tom continues writing.

"Tom, do you think it's possible to have a dream that's so intense you wake up thinking it's your real life?"

"Huh?"

"Yeah, me neither," I say.

He finally looks at me. "Ron, are you okay? You look terrible."

"I've been better."

"What's going on?"

"I lost my wife this morning."

"Oh my God." He rubs his forehead. "Jesus, Ron. I'm... I'm so sorry."

"She just disappeared. She was with me when I went to sleep and gone when I woke up. Didn't even leave a note."

"Oh..." He lets out a nervous chuckle. "Oh, okay. I thought you meant..."

I look blankly at him.

"Never mind," he says. "Any idea where she went?"

"None at all."

"Is she usually home when you wake up?"

"No."

"Oh…"

"She's usually at work already," I say.

"I see. So…"

"Yes, Tom. I checked to see if she was at work or not. She isn't. She's just gone."

"Wow. Okay. I'm sorry."

I nod.

"And she didn't leave you any explanation?" he asks.

"No, Tom. If she had, then she wouldn't be lost, would she?"

"No, I suppose not." He pushes his glasses up the bridge of his nose. "I guess I'm not following. Is she missing? Or did she leave you?"

"She's missing."

"Did you call the police? File a missing person's report?"

"It's a bit more complicated than that, I'm afraid."

"Really?" He scratches his head. "How so?"

"I'd prefer not to say. You'll think I'm crazy. Hell, I may just be. Brain tumor, perhaps. Who knows?"

Tom shifts his stance uncomfortably. "Ron, no offense, but you seem awfully calm about all this."

"I'm just trying to take it all in, you know? Wrap my head around it. It's a lot."

"Right, right. Well, I've never been married, so I'm no expert. But I have to say, if you truly believe your wife has disappeared, then you need to notify the police."

The police… They'll think I'm crazy too. And rightfully so. They'll probably have me checked into a mental facility by tomorrow morning. I'm sure this whole situation is just a big misunderstanding.

"You know what?" I say.

He raises his eyebrows. "What?"

I tap my hand against the desk. "I'm sure she's fine. It's obviously a prank. Knowing Kate, she probably set this whole thing up herself just to teach me a lesson." I laugh, a tinge hysterically. "Some kind of twisted anniversary present. It's certainly not out of the realm of possibilities. You know how women can be." I laugh harder.

Tom laughs with me, his eyes flicking from me to his clipboard to the door he entered through.

"I don't know why I didn't think of it sooner," I say. "It's just a test. One long, torturous test." My tone is serious now. Tom stops laughing, his expression mirroring mine. "I mean, how else would you explain this? A curse? That's not something that happens in the real world."

"Ron... I think—"

"It could be a curse, I suppose. Maybe God is punishing me for all the thoughts I had about Courtney yesterday. I'd deserve it too. That's what I get for picking up a strange woman at the train station, flirting with her, staring at her legs, imagining her as my wife..."

"Ron—"

"Lying in bed with her, kissing her in the room below where Kate was sleeping—"

"Ron!" Tom's voice pierces through my hysteria.

"What?"

"I think it would be in your best interest to go home and get your head straight. Take some time to figure all of this out. You're obviously under a lot of stress."

"But that's why I came here. To get my head straight. No, I need to stay here. Trust me, it's more stressful at home."

"It wasn't a suggestion, Ron. Get your stuff together and get out of here. That's an order."

I nod. "Fine…"

"Good. Let me know if you need anything. Take the rest of the week if you need it. Get some rest. You're probably just overworked."

"Thanks, Tom. You're a good guy, you know that?"

"Thanks, Ron," he says.

"No, I mean it. I'm not just saying that. I always thought you were a little uptight, but you're not so bad. We should hang out after work sometime. Grab a beer. Would that be inappropriate?"

He holds one hand up, stopping me from going down another stream of consciousness. "Just concentrate on getting your personal life straightened out, all right? You're no use to me like this. Call me tomorrow for an update, okay?"

I nod.

He opens the door and glances at me one last time before he leaves.

I study the photo again. I've looked at it every day for the last two years. It's the first thing I see when I sit and the last thing I see before I stand.

I grab the phone and dial Kate's parents; one of only a handful of numbers I have memorized.

"Hello?" A woman answers.

Thankfully, it sounds like Kate's mother.

"Martha?"

"Yes? Ron? Is that you?"

Relief washes over me. "Yeah, it's me."

"Oh, hi, Ron. I thought I recognized your voice. How are things at home? Are you and Courtney enjoying your time alone?"

The relief immediately washes away and gets replaced by sheer dread.

I close my eyes, her words penetrating my ears like a dull butter knife.

"Ron?"

"We're doing fine...thanks."

"Excellent. Got any special anniversary plans tonight? Going somewhere romantic?"

"Not sure yet." Suddenly my body feels too heavy to hold up on my own.

"Ron, are you okay? You don't sound like yourself."

"I'm fine," I lie. "I just miss the girls, that's all."

"Aw, I'm sure you do. Now you know how I feel between visits." She laughs. "Anyway, Lilly and Evelyn are at the store with their grandfather, but little Olivia is right here if you want to say hi?"

"Yes, please!" The weight is slightly lifted. "That would be great, thank you." I've never been more excited to hear someone's voice.

"All right, one moment."

Out of the three, Olivia looks the most like her mother with her curly brown hair and brown eyes. She even gets that cute crease between her eyes when she's concerned. She's like a mini-Kate.

She picks up the phone. "Hi, Daddy."

Her voice hasn't changed at all. Relief runs through me like a drug. My eyes fill with tears. "Hey, sweetie. How are you?"

"Good."

"What are you up to?"

"Making cookies with Grandma."

"Mm, that sounds good. Can I have one?"

She giggles. "No."

"How come?" I ask.

"Because you're too far away!" She giggles more.

I laugh. "Darn it. You're right." The sound of her sweet voice is like a balm to my aching soul.

"Daddy?"

"Yeah, honey?"

"Why *aren't* you and Mommy here?"

"Well, because this visit was just for you and your sisters. I have to stay here and work and take care of your mother." Great job I did there. "I'll see you when you get home though, okay?"

"Okay." Her voice is sad.

"You're having fun, aren't you?"

"Yeah…"

"And you're behaving yourself?"

"Uh-huh. I been good."

"Awesome. You'll be home in a few days, right?"

"Grandma?" she yells. "How many days till I go home?" She returns to the phone. "Three days."

"That's pretty soon." I breathe a sigh of relief.

"Is Mommy there?"

I lean my head toward my chest. "No, she's at work, honey."

"Okay."

"Do you miss her?" I ask.

"Uh-huh."

"Me too."

She giggles. "That's funny."

"It is, isn't it?"

"I drew a picture for Mommy today."

"You did?"

"Mm-hmm. It's got butterflies and flowers on it."

"Sounds beautiful. She'll love it."

"And lions too, 'cuz she likes lions, right Daddy?"

"Yup, she sure does..." Wait... Lions?

"And long green grass, and—"

"Wait, Olivia, did you say lions?"

"Yeah."

"You said Mommy likes lions?"

"Mm-hmm." She sounds frustrated with repeating herself, like it's the most obvious thing in the world.

Could it be?

"How do you know she likes lions? Is it because she has a collection of them at home?"

Her grandmother speaks in the background, but I can't make out what she's saying.

"Olivia?" She doesn't respond. "Olivia, Mommy has lion pajamas, right? Do you remember those?"

"Yay!" she yells and returns to the phone. "Gotta go, we're getting ice cream!"

"Wait, not yet!"

"Love you, Daddy." The call is disconnected.

Lions. It can't be a coincidence, can it? Maybe it is. Still, it feels like, through Olivia, I have made a small step toward finding Kate.

What am I going to do? How will the kids react when they return? Based on how things have gone so far, maybe they won't. Assuming they do, though, they'll probably come home and greet Courtney as the mother they've always known and loved. Last night, when I had this same thought, it seemed like an intriguing idea. Now the idea of Courtney sitting on the floor, playing games with the girls, inserting herself into a picture that isn't hers...it makes me want to throw up.

I pick up the phone and dial the number again.

No answer. I hang up.

I lean back in my chair and stare at the phone. Then, hoping for a miracle, I call Kate's cell phone. It rings once. Twice. Three times. The anticipation is overwhelming. My heart beats like a jackhammer.

Nobody answers. I hang up, feeling an enormous loss.

Tom walks by my office and points at me through the window, gesturing for me to leave. I nod.

I'm not ready to go home yet. I'm not ready to face the reality of what's there waiting for me.

I grab my bag and crawl underneath my desk, hugging my legs against my chest. I'll just sit for a while.

I rest my head on my knees and close my eyes...

When I open my eyes again, the room is darker. I slowly crawl out from under the desk and check the clock: 4:49 p.m. I sit down in my chair for a moment and then I pick up the phone and call the house. After three rings, someone answers. "Hello?"

It's Courtney.

"Hey, it's me," I say.

"Hey. It's good to hear your voice," she says, sounding tentative but relieved. Oddly enough, it's good to hear her voice too. "How are you? Are you feeling any better?"

"I honestly have no idea. It fluctuates, minute by minute."

"That's okay. There's no rush. How did it go at work? Did you find what you were looking for?"

"No, not exactly."

We're both silent for a moment.

"I'm sorry," she says. "Do you want to come home?"

"Yeah. I think maybe I do."

"And...you want me to be here too?"

I think about it for a second. The thought of being alone right now feels unbearable. "Yes."

"Great," she says, relief coloring her voice. "It's too quiet in this house without you."

I nod.

"Well, I'll be here, waiting for you."

"Okay. I'm sorry if I was harsh this morning. I'm sorry I yelled at you."

"Oh, that's okay. Don't even worry about that. I'm just glad you're feeling better."

I start to hang up.

"Ron?"

"Yeah?"

"Do you still want to go out to dinner tonight? It doesn't need to be anywhere fancy. Just someplace quiet where we can sit and talk. I think it would be good for us. Change of scenery, you know?"

"Sure. That sounds nice. Thanks, Courtney."

"You got it. I've got the perfect place in mind. I'll drive, so you can just relax. Abby next door already said I could borrow her car."

I sit silently, lost in thought.

"In fact," she says, "how about I make it really easy and come get you? That way you can skip the hassle of the trains."

"No, that's not necessary. I appreciate the offer, though."

"Are you sure? I don't mind. I can be there in forty-five minutes. We'll eat right there in the city so you don't have to wait."

"Yeah, I'm sure. I may take another quick nap on the train. I'm exhausted. I'm hoping with a little more rest, I'll feel even better."

"All right," she says. "I love you, Ron."

"I'll see you soon." I hang up and leave my office.

At the train station, I wait for ten minutes on the platform before realizing that my train won't arrive for another half hour. Lacking anything productive to do, I wander into a jewelry store that sits just inside the station. I browse for a couple of minutes before stumbling across a pair of diamond earrings with lime green gemstone carved lions at the center of them. I take a closer look. They're peridot gemstones. Kate's birthstone. Lion-shaped peridot gemstones. It has to be a sign.

The cashier places the earrings in a gift box, and I accept it without a bag, sliding it into my pocket for safe keeping. The earrings would be a perfect anniversary present for Kate.

A homesick feeling aches inside my gut.

I miss her.

As I exit the store and wander back to my platform, I try to wrap my mind around the fact that I may never find Kate. Never look into her eyes. Hold her hands. Kiss her lips... I can't do it. I'm not interested in a world without Kate. I hate myself for pushing her so far away and for even entertaining the idea that I might be better off without her. I can't believe that just last night I thought divorce was the best answer. I need Kate.

So, where is she?

There's got to be more I can do. I should have searched the house better. There must be something... Wait. That's it. I'm such an idiot. I just have to search the house more. We keep our marriage license in the safe. I can check that. That alone will solve the mystery. What else? The attic? Boxes loaded with twelve years' worth of stuff. I'll ask to see Courtney's driver's license for proof of who she is. Why didn't I think of this stuff when I was home this morning? I was in shock. I wasn't thinking clearly. But now I am. I can make more phone calls too. Friends. Hell, our neighbors, Abby and Tim, will know.

I feel better already.

Still though… I'm almost afraid to learn the truth. What if the evidence proves that Courtney was telling the truth? That she is my real wife. What then? I hate to even think of it.

Courtney will just have to be patient with me while I work this out. She's been pretty understanding so far, if she *is* telling the truth, that is. She's certainly not the worst wife Kate could've switched places with. But how can I be happy with someone I barely know? I don't know any of the little details that accumulate throughout years of marriage. What's her favorite ice cream? What type of movies does she like to watch? Does she cry when she watches *Old Yeller*? Will she remember that Lilly takes an allergy pill and two inhalers before bed every night? Does she cook? Is she caring? What are her hobbies? Will she be there for me when it counts? Kate always was. She may be rough around the edges, with attitude to spare, but at the end of the day, I always knew she had my back no matter what. Isn't that what true love is?

I need to get to the train and go to sleep as soon as possible. That's where I'm most likely to find Kate again, sadly. I don't want it to be true, but right now it's all I have.

I step aboard the train, on the verge of tears. What am I going to do about dinner tonight? I don't know what to say or how to act around Courtney. I wish I could crawl into a hole and disappear. Curl up and sleep until everything is back to normal.

I take the first window seat I find, avoiding eye contact with everyone I pass along the way.

A young boy sitting across from me has a small black backpack on his lap with tiny stars all over it.

I think of the night I went to visit Kate at The Satellite Restaurant, where she worked. It was only the second time I'd spoken to her.

I lean back, close my eyes, and picture Kate in my head. I've heard that if you think about someone hard enough before you go to sleep, the more likely you are to dream about them.

I stumble into another dream. I'm back in some war-torn country, this time trying to protect Kate from terrorists. The two of us are hiding inside somebody else's house. It's small and cluttered. Kate is scared. I hold her close and promise to keep her safe. A hooded figure walks into the room holding a large gun. We crouch behind a counter. I hear heavy footsteps approaching and hold my breath, praying that we won't be discovered. Then I feel the barrel of the gun pressing against the back of my head. The trigger releases a slight squeak as the hooded figure pulls it back, and I know I'm about to die. This is the end. But...no, this can't be the end. What am I doing? I have a wife to protect and three daughters waiting for us at home. I can't just lie down and die. It's my job to be there for her. I jump up, spin around, and grab the neck of the gun. The hazel eyes in the shadow of the hood are eerily familiar.

"Courtney?" I ask.

She wrenches the gun from my fingers and points it at Kate. A buzzing noise emerges from the gun. I jump between them as she pulls the trigger. Pain strikes my gut, but only a little, and then everything goes dark.

CHAPTER THIRTEEN

THE SATELLITE RESTAURANT, 1989

A few days after I met Kate at the bookstore, I decided to drop by The Satellite for a visit. It was a Tuesday evening, and it was hot.

I sat in a booth and waited, unsure if she would even be there. A waiter arrived to take my order, and I asked him if Kate was working. A couple of minutes later she appeared in front of me, all smiles. She took my breath away almost instantly.

She sat with me for longer than was allowed, sharing an order of buffalo wings with me. She was right; they were pretty amazing. I caught her supervisor throwing angry glances at her once or twice, but she didn't seem to care, so neither did I.

"What I really want to do is get into politics," she said. She raised her voice so I could hear her over both the music and the crowd.

"What kind of politics?" I asked.

She leaned forward and sipped her pink lemonade through a straw. "President of the United States, of course."

I laughed.

The skin in her forehead creased. "What?"

"Nothing... Sorry, I didn't mean to laugh like that. It's a great idea. It just wasn't what I was expecting you to say."

She smiled. "No?"

"No. But, I admire your ambition. It's always good to aim high, right?"

"That's right! Like the Air Force."

"Is that what they do?" I asked.

She nodded. "Mm-hmm."

"Why, because they fly planes?"

She shrugged her shoulders. "Beats me. That's just what my dad taught me. That and they always say that on the commercials."

"Your dad was in the Air Force?"

"No, Army. But he sure liked to make fun of the Air Force a lot." She cupped her hand around her mouth like she was telling a secret. "I think he was just jealous, though."

"What's that like? Having a parent in the military?"

She took a moment to think about it. "Lonely."

Again, not the answer I was expecting.

"Why? Was he gone a lot?"

She cleared her throat and took another sip of her lemonade. "How's your strawberry shake?"

I took a sip. "Delicious."

She smiled.

We sat quietly for a bit, listening to the voices around us.

"What's your plan B?" I asked.

She raised an eyebrow.

"If politics doesn't work out?"

She swirled her straw around inside her cup. "Real estate. You?"

"Rocket Science."

A huge smile spread across her face, front teeth and all. And in that moment, sitting there with her, she made me feel like I was someone special. I thought about how easy it would be to spend hours listening to her talk. I couldn't wait to learn more.

After we finished our drinks, she walked me out to my car.

"I hope I didn't get you fired," I said to her.

"Doubt it. I'm the only thing that keeps this place hopping most nights."

I thought of the other waiters and waitresses, older men and women with dried up smiles, and nodded decisively. "I believe that."

When I got to my car, I turned and looked at her, my gut boiling over with anticipation.

"So? What did you think?" she asked.

In my mind I responded, "I think I'm already falling in love with you." With my mouth, I responded, "Of the restaurant?"

She nodded shyly and bit down on the corner of her bottom lip. "Mm-hmm."

I glanced back at the restaurant. "It's great. I thoroughly enjoyed it." What I was really referring to was my time with her. The conversation we had. I honestly couldn't remember what the food even tasted like. "Seems like a pretty cool place to work."

She shrugged. "Yeah, I guess." She ran her hand through her hair, then looked at me with serious eyes. "I will be something someday, you know. Something amazing, even."

I felt my heart melt down through my ribcage. "I have no doubt," I said. "In fact, I already think you're amazing."

Her face lit up like I had just lifted her up and gently placed her on top of the world.

I put my hand on her face and caressed her cheek with my thumb. She closed her eyes and leaned into it. Her cheek grew warm against my fingers. Then she looked at me and said, "You're sweet." She held my hand in place for a moment, then she brought our hands down together, making sure I remained firmly in her grip, rubbing the top of my hand with her thumb. "I've got big plans. I'd love to tell you more about them some-time, if you're interested. Maybe over coffee or something."

"Yeah, sure, that'd be great," I said. "How about Thursday night? I'll take you to The Silver Key Diner. It's my favorite. That's your day off, right?"

She blushed. "Yeah. I can't believe you remembered my schedule."

"Oh, I remember, all right."

She laughed. "Sorry I'm not off on a better day. I know Thursday's probably not very convenient."

"No, it's perfect. I'd much rather go before the weekend when it's quiet." I don't want to miss a word she says, I thought.

"All right then, it's a date," she said.

"Great." We both grinned. "It doesn't have any stars on the walls or anything, though. Hope that's okay."

She laughed. "I don't know, that's pretty unacceptable. But, I suppose I can live with that." She winked.

"We'll get dinner. And talk."

"Sounds perfect," said Kate. She blinked, and like magic, her eyes sparkled, reflecting both the stars and the moon. It was all right there. An entire galaxy of hopes and dreams resting comfortably in her eyes.

CHAPTER FOURTEEN

DEJA VU

I wake with such a strong jolt that my hand hits the arm of the person next to me.

"Whoa!" says a heart-wrenchingly familiar voice.

Without even looking, I know it's Kate.

I hold my breath as I slowly turn my head toward her. Our eyes meet and chills run up and down my spine. It's her. It's really her. Kate is sitting next to me, dressed in semi-casual clothes—jeans and a black leather jacket over a button-up blouse. I don't recognize any of the clothing, but everything else about her is just as I remember.

She cocks one eyebrow, her e-reader gripped firmly in her hands. "Everything all right?"

Is this real? Is she real? She has to be. I want to grab her and kiss her and tell her how wonderful it is to see her. But her face shows no signs of recognition. And if she really doesn't know me, I need to choose my words and actions carefully, so I don't scare her off.

"Yeah. Sorry... I was dreaming."

"I'll say." She sets her tablet down on her lap. "Was it one of those stressful dreams where you're constantly running or hiding from someone, but you can never quite get away?"

I sit up straight. "Yeah, just like that, actually."

I want to tell her how she was in it, and how I protected her, but I know I can't.

"Those are the worst," she says. "When you can never run fast enough. And every time you think you've found a clever hiding spot, they still find you."

I nod. "Exactly. You're good."

"Actually, I'm Kate." She holds out her right hand and smiles.

I shake her hand, thrilled to be touching her once again. "Ron." I glance down at her other hand. No wedding ring.

"Hi, Ron."

She's so beautiful. Good God, I missed her. And to think, she's only been gone for a few hours. It feels like a lifetime.

She smiles and then turns her attention back to whatever she's reading. I slip my wedding ring off and stick it in my pocket. I need to hear her voice more. I need to look at her. My eyes brim with tears as I try not to stare. She glances over at me, gives me another quick smile, and returns her eyes to her book.

"I didn't hurt you, did I?" I blurt out, desperate to keep the conversation going.

She looks at me with that classic crease of concern forming between her brows. "Hurt me?"

"I hit your arm when I woke up. Are you okay?"

"Oh…" She blushes. "Yes, I'm fine, thanks. You didn't hurt me at all. I'm quite durable."

I turn to stare out the window, suddenly overwhelmed. Overwhelmed with the joy of seeing her again, but also overwhelmed with the idea that she doesn't know who I am. In her eyes, I'm a complete stranger.

"How about you?" she asks. "Are you okay?"

I look back at her. "Yeah. I am now, thanks. It's been a rough day." I have no idea how to explain any of this.

She adjusts her position in the seat and sighs. "Yeah, I've had plenty of those myself."

The voice on the speaker announces our stop.

We grab our stuff, prepared to stand.

"You get off here too?" she asks.

"I do, yes."

"Hmm. I'm surprised I've never seen you before."

"No more than I."

The train stops. We exit and head to the parking garage together.

"You do look a little familiar," she says. "Do I look familiar to you?"

I place my hand over my pocket, feeling the box-shaped lump that rests inside. "I've seen you around."

She cocks her head. "You have?"

"Definitely."

We come to the crosswalk outside the parking garage. Panic sets in. It's almost time to go our separate ways. What am I going to do?

I reach into my pocket and squeeze the box tight. The light changes, and we proceed across the road.

Walking up the stairs, sharp pains strike my chest in time with my pounding heartbeat. She stops at the second-floor door and turns to look at me.

"Well, it's been a pleasure, Ron."

"It certainly has."

She tilts her head endearingly. "Maybe I'll run into you again sometime?"

"I'd like that very much."

She smiles big, showing off her perfect white teeth. A lump forms in my throat. She studies my face like she's trying to figure me out, and I study hers like I've never seen it before and need to memorize every gorgeous detail.

We both laugh for no reason.

A million words sit silently on the tip of my tongue, eager to carry my feelings to her ears. But I can't organize them fast enough to justify letting them go. She pushes the door open, slips through it, and disappears.

Up on the third floor, I walk to my car feeling as though I've been torn open. Like something inside of me is missing. Something essential. When I was in this same situation yesterday, walking along this same floor, I was anxious and bursting with renewed excitement. Now that excitement is replaced with a deep longing. A homesick type of sadness again. The key to my happiness is within my grasp, it has been for years, and somehow it's still too far to grab ahold of.

Then it hits me: I let her get away.

Why didn't I at least ask for her number? What if that was my only chance? What if I never see her again? She's probably going home to her boyfriend. Or fiancé. Or husband! Not everyone wears their wedding ring every day. My body trembles at the thought.

I start my car and switch the stereo off before it can blast me. I take the turns through the parking garage slowly, still shaky and trying desperately to keep it together. When I reach the second level, I spot her up ahead and hit the brakes. I can't believe my eyes. There she is, leaning down under the hood of her car, the same way Courtney was yesterday.

I pull up behind her and roll my window down. "Hey."

She looks up, startled. "Oh, hey. It's you."

"Sorry, I didn't mean to scare you."

"No, it's fine. Perfect timing, actually." She gestures under the hood.

"Car trouble?"

"It seems that way, yes." She looks down and lowers her eyebrows. "Nice door..."

"Thanks. I did it myself."

She smirks. "I don't suppose you know anything about cars? Apart from crashing them, that is."

"I know you have to turn it on and put it in drive before it will move forward." She chuckles under her breath. "Is that the kind of knowledge you're looking for?"

"No, I'm afraid not," she says.

"Darn. Well, in that case... I know nothing. Sorry," I say, frowning.

"It's okay. I appreciate your honesty." She glances at the engine. "Would you mind taking a quick look anyway?"

I smile.

"Couldn't hurt, right?" she continues. "You can't possibly know less than me."

"Sure, I'd be happy to. Just don't get your hopes up."

I park in the closest available spot and take a deep breath before leaving the car, trying to follow my own advice. I don't know what's going on yet, or what any of this means, but I *do* know I have her within my grasp, and that's everything. Nothing else matters. Hell, she may even need a ride home. We'll have a chance to talk and get to know each other again. It'll be like old times. The problem is, we forgot how to talk to each other. We forgot why we fell in love in the first place. I know I can fix the damage I've done. I'll do whatever it takes to hold on to her for good. To take care of her and appreciate her the way she deserves.

I check under her hood. As expected, everything appears normal, at least to my eyes. Nothing's sparking or visibly on fire.

"What was wrong with it initially? It wouldn't start?"

She shakes her head. "Nope."

"Did it make any noise when you turned the key?"

She puffs her breath through her lips. "Yeah, at first. But then nothing."

"Well, if it was silent, then it's most likely your battery. Which is a good thing."

"Gotcha. That doesn't sound so bad. See, you do know some stuff."

I shrug. "Just the basics, I guess."

"Do you have any jumper cable thingies?"

"I do, actually." One of the few things I know how to use on a car.

"Cool. Would you mind giving me a jump?" She tucks her hair behind her ears and smiles sweetly.

I feel my cheeks go red. "I'd love to."

I grab the cables from my trunk, and after a few false starts, her engine hums back to life.

"Awesome!" she says. She steps out of her car and does a tiny celebratory jump, pumping her fists.

We lean, side by side, against the front of her car. She raises her hand and we give each other a high five.

"Nice work," she says. "I guess it *was* the battery, after all."

"I guess it was."

"Thanks for the jump, Ron. You're a lifesaver."

"My pleasure."

"I owe you one."

"A jump?" I ask, offering her a cheeky grin.

She raises one eyebrow. "Let's not get carried away. You haven't even asked me out to dinner yet."

"May I?" My heart sings inside my chest.

"May you what? Ask me out?"

"Yes. I'd like that very much."

"Would you?" She crosses her arms, her eyes scanning my face, searching for hidden agendas. "Sure. You can ask. As long as you don't expect me to say yes."

I scratch my head.

"I'm kidding," she says. "When?"

My gut tingles with anticipation. "How about right now?"

"You don't waste time, do you?"

"Can't afford to. Life is too short."

She nods thoughtfully, biting down on her bottom lip. "Well, it's a little short notice, but…what the hell?"

"Really? You will?"

"Sure, why not? I was going to go home and make myself dinner, but it's just leftovers, and to be honest, I'm not very hungry. What did you have in mind?"

"If you're not hungry, we could just have coffee and chat at the Silver Key Diner downtown. You like coffee?"

"Love it," she says. "Too much, probably."

I nod and smile.

She taps her bottom lip with her index finger. "Coffee and chat, huh?" She studies me intently. "Sounds fairly harmless. Unless, of course, you're a serial killer."

I snort. "Do I look like a serial killer?"

"Maybe. They're known to be quite charming. Until they no longer need to be, that is."

"Kind of like when people change after marriage."

"Exactly," she says.

"Well, you're in luck, because I'm only slightly charming, and I've never harmed anyone before."

"Sounds promising."

"I'll take good care of you."

"Good," she says. "That's what I like to hear."

"Besides," I continue with a grin, "something tells me that you can hold your own."

"Smart man."

CHAPTER FIFTEEN

HAPPY ANNIVERSARY

Kate drives herself to the diner, keeping in sight of my car. As I pull into a parking space, I notice my jacket on the floor of the back seat and grab it. I'll bring it with me in case she gets cold. We make our way inside and seat ourselves toward the back of the diner. The atmosphere is relaxed and quiet, unlike my heart which is currently anything but...

Kate mumbles under her breath while she digs through her purse, looking for something. "Shit..." she mutters. "I swear, if I end up with one more stupid discount card..." She looks up at me, as if she's just now realizing she's not the only one in the room. "Sorry, I know I'm talking to myself. I must sound ridiculous."

I smile warmly at her. "Not at all. I think you sound great."

She pulls out a small tube of lip gloss and applies it to her lips. "Yeah, adorable, I'm sure. You wouldn't think so if you lived with me, believe me."

I open my mouth, prepared to argue, but decide against it.

She rubs her shiny lips together, and I fight the urge to lean across the table and kiss her. I grab my legs under the table and remind myself of how horrible an idea that would be. I have to be patient, or I'll lose her forever.

She tosses the lip gloss into her purse and takes one more peek inside of it. "I left my phone at home this morning…" She closes the purse and sets it on the seat next to her. "It's got me feeling all out of sorts today."

"Funny you should say that. I did the same thing."

"Really?" Her nose scrunches up. "That *is* funny."

I glance around the room, at this diner where we fell in love during our first date, fourteen years ago. We sat in this exact same seat, at the same cherry red table.

"You been here before?" Kate asks.

I smile, a tad mischievously, because I know things that she doesn't. She blushes, and after a moment she leans her elbows on the table and cups her face with her hands. She's trying to hide the blush, embarrassed by how easily it rises.

"I certainly have," I say. "It's been a while, though. You?"

She shakes her head, looking at me thoughtfully.

A blonde-haired waitress comes by and sets two cups of coffee down on the table. She looks at us with a practiced customer service smile and empty eyes, and asks us if we'd like anything else. We decline.

I grab us a few packets of cream and sugar and take the liberty of preparing both of our coffees. Kate looks at me like I'm crazy.

I glance at her. "Lots of cream, a little sugar, right?"

"Uh…yes, Ron. That's correct. Thanks for being creepy and knowing that already."

"My pleasure," I say, grinning. I stir both cups and set hers down in front of her. "There you go."

"Thank you." She picks it up with both hands, looks at me skeptically, and takes a long sip. It's amazing how relaxed she seems. I hadn't realized just how much we'd changed over the years.

Her face relaxes as she finishes with her sip, and a smile curls her lips.

"Well?" I say.

"It's perfect, thank you. No one ever gets my coffee right."

"You're welcome."

It's amazing. Already, I can feel the electricity running between us. I wonder if she feels it too. It's taking every bit of strength I have not to leap over this table and embrace her.

She sets the cup down and clears her throat. "So, Ron. What the hell is going on with you today?"

"What do you mean?"

"I mean, are you having a midlife crisis or something? Worst day of your life? Tell me what's got you looking so disheveled."

"What makes you think I don't always look this way?"

She shrugs. "Just a hunch, I guess."

I lean forward, with my elbows on the table. "Kate... What do you see when you look at me?"

"Is this a trick question?"

"No."

She studies my face for a couple of seconds. "A man who's having a midlife crisis."

"That's it?"

"For now, yeah."

"May I be blunt with you?" I ask, realizing that I no longer feel nervous. Hopefully that's not a bad sign.

"Sure. It's been working pretty well for you so far, hasn't it?"

"I don't know, has it?"

"I'm sitting here with you, aren't I?"

I drum my fingers on the table, allowing my eyes to linger on her. "Do you find me attractive?"

She looks away. "Oh, boy."

"I'm serious."

"Are you always like this on a first date?" She glances around the room suspiciously. "Is this some kind of prank?"

"No."

"It has to be. Everything about this is weird. Seriously, where's the hidden camera?"

I chuckle. "It's not a prank. Not that I know of, at least. If it is, then it's on both of us."

"Huh?"

"Look, I understand this is a bit strange, but I need you to just go with it, okay? It'll be fun. Think of it as a game, or an experimental new way of getting to know someone."

She raises an eyebrow.

"And I promise to tell the truth," I say.

"The whole truth?"

"The whole truth."

"And nothing but the truth?"

"Right," I say.

"In a court of law?"

"In a court of law. And also here in this diner." I smile.

"Good answer," she says. She sips her coffee. "Lucky for you, I find you oddly charming." She takes another sip, giving me a long, hard look, and then sets her mug down definitively.

"All right, Ron. I'll give you the benefit of the doubt. I've gotta know where this is going."

"Great." I breathe a sigh of relief.

She blushes, then looks away briefly. Maybe our chemistry has faded over the years, but right now, in this diner, it's just as strong as it was the first time we sat together at this table.

"So, where were we again?" she asks.

"I asked if you find me attractive."

"Oh, right, right." She takes another long breath, like she has to think really hard about it. "Yeah, I suppose you meet the threshold."

"The threshold? What's that supposed to mean?"

"You know, it means... Well... Never mind. Perhaps that wasn't the best way to put it."

"I certainly hope not."

"Let me try this again," she says.

"Okay."

"Yes, I would say you qualify as attractive."

"I qualify?" I cock one eyebrow at her.

"Yes."

"You sure have a way with words. You're not a poet by any chance, are you?"

She points at me. "Shut it."

"Well, thanks...I guess."

"No sweat. Just don't let it go to your head."

"I don't see how it could."

"I wouldn't sleep with you or anything, if that's what you're asking."

"Wow," I say. "That was blunt."

"Hey, you set the rules. You asked me to roll with the punches. I can roll with the best of 'em."

"Okay, fair enough. So you wouldn't sleep with me."

She shakes her head. "Nope."

"But you would marry me and have children with me?"

"Absolutely not."

"Why not?"

"I just said I wouldn't sleep with you."

"So?"

"So," she says. "It's even more unlikely that I would marry you or have children with you, don't you think? I mean, one generally leads to the other." She puts her hand over her mouth in mock horror. "Oh my God! Your parents never had that talk with you, did they? I'm so sorry."

There's that sarcasm I grew to both love and hate over the years.

I take my wedding ring back out of my pocket and slip it back on my finger, underneath the table so she doesn't see it yet.

"I'm willing to bet that if you spent enough time with me, then you'd eventually change your mind and want to marry me, and have kids, and spend the rest of your life with me," I retort.

"I doubt it," she says. "Anyways, I don't want kids of my own. I prefer to enjoy other people's kids. Much less responsibility, with the same amount of fun."

"That's right, I forgot about that." She told me that on our original first date, as well.

I rest my hands on the table.

"Say what?" she asks, perplexed. Then she glances down at my hand. "Is that a wedding ring on your finger?"

I look at it, moving it back and forth with my thumb. "It is."

"So, you're married?"

"Yeah."

"Currently?" she asks, incredulity in her voice.

"Yes."

"You're not even divorced or anything? Separated? Trial separation, maybe?"

"Well…" How can I explain this without sounding like an ass?

She crosses her arms over her chest, frowning. I know that look. It means I'm in trouble, and I'd better think fast.

"I should have known—"

"It's not what you think," I say.

"Sure it isn't." She grabs her purse and throws it over her shoulder. "It was nice meeting you, Ron. Thanks for the jump." She makes as if to rise.

I place my hand down on the table. "It isn't. I promise. We were separated recently."

"I don't believe you. How long?"

I rub my eyes, remembering how I promised to tell the truth. "Approximately…one day." I smile uncomfortably.

She glares at me like she's trying to set me on fire. If anyone could do that, it'd be Kate. "Cute. Really cute."

"Listen," I say. "I know what you're thinking, but please don't leave without hearing me out first."

She sits there silently, arms still crossed, eyes masked with distrust, most likely weighing her options.

"Please?" I beg.

She sets her bag back down on the seat. "You don't know what I'm thinking. Nor do you want to."

"I think I have a pretty good idea."

"All right then, enlighten me."

"Well, I know you think I'm a scumbag right now."

She nods. "That's true. Not necessarily the word I would have used, but yes, you're right."

"But the thing is, you wouldn't if you knew who I was married to."

She narrows her eyes. "I don't see how that could possibly make any difference."

"Hear me out and you will."

She turns her face away.

"Come on," I say. "You said you'd play along, right?"

Her eyes snap back to me.

"Just give me five more minutes. That's all I ask. What's the worst that could happen?"

She relaxes her shoulders. "All right, I'm listening. To whom are you married?"

I pause and take a deep breath before answering.

Here it goes... No turning back now.

"To you," I say.

Her eyes go wide, and the sarcasm is evident in her tone. "Really?"

"Yes."

"Fascinating."

"Isn't it?"

"Quite. You promised to tell the truth, remember?"

"I remember."

She looks me up and down. "If that's true, then where's my ring?"

"You don't have one yet," I tell her.

"Why not?"

"Because we're not actually married yet. I mean, we are. Just not...yet, I guess." I scratch my head nervously. "It's really hard to explain. I hardly understand it myself."

"Apparently."

"I mean, obviously, you're not married to me right now, at this very moment, as you are now. But we *are* married, you just don't know it yet. That's where I come in."

"I have to say, this is, without a doubt, the most creative pickup line a guy has ever tried on me."

I lean forward and look her in the eye, urging her to understand how serious I am. "It's not a line."

Her sarcastic smile simmers down a few degrees. "If we're not married right now, at this very moment, as I am now, then when?" she asks.

"Well, now, but in some sort of alternative timeline."

She raises an eyebrow.

"In fact, today's our anniversary."

"Is it?"

"Yes." I smile. "It is. Twelve years."

"Twelve years?"

"Twelve years. Not bad, huh?"

"Married twelve years in a parallel universe."

I nod, thoughtfully. "Mm-hmm."

She shrugs her shoulders and nods. "Okay."

"Okay?"

"Sure, why not?"

"Great!" I say, relieved.

"I mean, what fun is life if you don't take a chance and run with a completely insane, impossible idea once in a while? Right?"

"Right."

She rubs her finger along the top of her coffee mug, all the way around. Then she presses her fingertip to her lips, tasting the tiny drop of coffee she'd rounded up and captured, looking at me with those curious, endearing brown eyes of hers. "So, you're like what? A time traveler or something?"

"Something like that, yeah. That's not a bad way of looking at it."

"Like Marty McFly?"

I smile. "Yes, like Marty McFly."

"So, then that makes me like your Doc Brown, right?"

"Uh...no, gross."

"Not Doc Brown, I meant..." She snaps her fingers. "Loraine! I'm your Loraine."

"Ooh, wrong again. Even grosser, I'm afraid."

"What do you mean?" she asks.

"Loraine is Marty's mother."

"What? Are you sure?"

"One hundred percent positive."

"Yeah, you're right. I'm definitely not your mother. At least, I hope not. How old are you again?"

"You never were very good at remembering movie details."

"I'm not sure how you would know that, but I don't appreciate you picking on me," she mutters, looking sulky again. Already, she's having trouble hiding her sensitive side.

"Sorry," I say.

"Picking on me will make me want to get up and leave. And to be honest, I'm not sure why I haven't done that already."

Crap, I'm losing her again. "Very sorry," I say. "It won't happen again. If it helps, you're amazing at remembering important details from real life!"

"Mm-hmm. So, who am I, in this *Back to the Future* metaphor of yours?"

"You mean analogy?"

"No, I mean metaphor… I think I do. Don't I?" she asks half to herself, placing her hand on mine as she considers it. After a moment, she realizes what she's doing and pulls away.

I lean back and sigh. "I suppose you would be my Jennifer."

"Isn't that the chick that sleeps through the whole movie?"

"Yeah, sort of. But only in the sequel. That's not the point, though."

"What *is* the point?"

I lean forward. "That he *had* to put her to sleep in order to protect her, because he loves her. That's the point."

"Ah… I see." She nods slowly, giving me another good, hard look. "So, how is this future marriage of ours, anyway? Do we get along well?"

I scratch the back of my head nervously. "It's complicated."

"Is it?" Her head tips to the side in that endearing way she has.

"Very."

"Tell me about it."

"Like, you agree with me? Or you literally want me to tell you about it?"

"I mean literally tell me about it. I want to hear about our marriage. Our future marriage that hasn't happened yet. The one I know nothing about, but you seem to remember perfectly. I want to hear about that one, specifically."

I raise my eyebrows. "Has anyone ever told you that you have a way with words?"

She blows against her bangs with force. "You have no idea."

Our argument in the kitchen yesterday resurfaces in my mind, followed by our fight before bed last night. I hear her voice again, saying *I need more from you, Ron.* I have to make this good. I have to give her everything I've got, everything I'm capable of, if I want to hold on to her for good this time.

"I beg to differ," I say.

"Do you?"

"I do."

She waves one hand languidly. "No need to beg. Please, differ away. Tell me what you know about me. About us."

"You're not seeing anyone currently, are you?"

She gives me a blank stare. "All of a sudden you're concerned about that?"

"I probably should have asked that already, huh?"

"You think?"

"Well, are you?" I ask again.

"No. Men are a big pain in the ass. I generally try to avoid them as much as possible."

"Okay, good." Relief rolls through me.

"Do you really think I'd be sitting here with you if I was?"

I shrug. "I don't know, maybe. Depends."

"On what?"

"The circumstances. Maybe you're not happy. Maybe you're looking for something more, but you're not sure what it is?"

"Is that what you're doing?" she asks.

"No. I know exactly what I'm looking for."

We stare at each other. I risk a smile, but her face remains serious. Close to it, at least. She wants to smile, but won't allow herself to. She's stubborn like that. I've seen it so many times, the effort in her eyes as she tries to force her face into line. But when she wants to smile bad enough, like she does right now, it always finds a way to emerge. Oftentimes, our heart is stronger than our will.

"Our marriage. Start talking," she commands.

"Well... First of all, we love each other. A lot. That's the most important part."

"Mm-hmm," she says, sipping her coffee again.

"But, sometimes we forget to show it. And when that happens, we argue."

"How unfortunate," she says in her driest tone. "Doesn't sound too bad, though."

"It's not."

We stare at each other for a few seconds.

"I'm very high maintenance," she says.

"I know."

"And emotional."

"I know."

"I feel a lot."

"I know. That's one of the reasons I love you so much."

She blushes. "And I get cranky," she says, making her best serious face for more effect.

"That's an understatement," I say.

"But I'm worth it."

"Absolutely. You know, I'm not sure if I've told you this before, but I love that little crinkle that forms between your brows whenever you're confused or concerned, like right now."

She rubs her finger between her eyes self-consciously.

"It's adorable," I say.

She brings her hand down. "I'm not adorable. And you're not impressing me. What else you got?"

"You're crankiest when you're tired."

"You mean like every other human on the planet?"

"Your favorite color is purple."

Kate quirks her lips and shrugs. "Debatable."

"You love lions. They're your favorite animal."

She nods. "Better…"

"Seriously, you *love* them. Someday you'll have a large collection of lion-related items, if you don't already. Your idea of a perfect day is a warm walk on the beach and browsing through the little shops around the harbor. You tend to sleep on your side, preferably with a wall behind you. You don't like having too much empty space next to you. Even when you're mad at me, you hate sleeping alone. You're very cuddly but also get hot easily, so you're often conflicted between the two."

I pause for a moment, curious if she'll try to deny any of it. She doesn't. She appears to be listening intently.

"You love the Rolling Stones," I continue. "But you don't tell most people because you don't want to start a debate over whether they're better than The Beatles. You love the movie *Old Yeller*, but hate that it makes you cry every time you watch it. You have a habit of saying 'supposably' instead of 'supposedly.'" I take a moment to think of another good fact. Something meaningful. "When you were little you wanted to be a princess. And all those Disney cartoons convinced you it was possible. But, as an adult, you learned the difference between fairy tales and reality. Occasionally you think back on that dream with sadness, and feel like a fool for ever believing it."

"Are you done?" she asks, her voice cracking a little. Her eyes are wet with tears, but she hasn't let them fall yet.

"Almost. You like your job well enough, but you love drawing more, and if you had it your way, you'd make a living at it. But you can't seem to organize yourself enough to figure out how to go about it. People at your job perceive you as being very tough, and you can be when you have to be, but you're actually quite sensitive. You don't like that about yourself, though, so you keep it hidden, pretending to be tougher than you are because you were hurt too many times during your childhood."

"That's enough," she says.

I smile.

She smiles back, her eyes glistening. "How many perfect days on the beach have you taken me on?"

"Not enough."

"How many is not enough?"

I purse my lips and puff out my cheeks. "Mm... A handful, maybe."

"You're right, that's not enough," she says.

"I know. I'm going to make it up to you, though."

She takes her last sip of coffee. "Well, you've certainly said a lot. More than I was initially willing to give you credit for. Now, let me ask *you* something."

"Sure, anything."

"What's important to you?"

I bite down on the corner of my lip and smile, my mind flashing through the events of the past couple of days. "It's funny... If you had asked me that a week ago, my answer would probably be very different. But recently I've had a chance to re-evaluate my life, and I think I now have a much better understanding of what's important to me."

"Great. Let's hear it."

"What's most important to me, above all else, is you and our beautiful daughters. Our family. Being the best husband and father I can be. Taking care of you the way you deserve. Loving you and appreciating you and listening to your problems. Because I love you, and I feel blessed that you love me too. I want to make you feel like the amazing woman you are. Because that's my job, and I'm privileged to have it. I never want to take you for granted. I want to communicate better, even when I'm feeling frustrated or withdrawn. I want to do everything in my power to make sure you never, ever feel alone." I reach across the table and take her hands in mine.

"That's a pretty good answer," she says.

We both laugh under our breath.

She looks down at the table. "Are you sure we have kids?"

"Positive."

"But I told you I don't even want kids."

"But you will. And you should. You're an amazing mother. The best, actually. Not to mention we make awesome kids."

"How many are we talking?"

"Three."

"Jesus."

"I know."

"What the hell were we thinking?" she asks. I grin at the familiar phrase and squeeze her hands in mine.

"That we had a lot of love to give."

"No wonder we argue."

"It's a lot of work. But someday they'll grow up."

"That's generally how it works."

"And move out."

"God willing."

"And then all we'll have is each other."

"Oh, my. Sounds scary." She squeezes my hands. "What then?" she asks, the dramatic flair in her voice failing to mask her real curiosity.

I lean in close, and she does the same, our hands gripped together tightly.

"It will be wonderful," I say, "because I'll take care of you for the rest of your life. And we'll be happy together. We'll cherish our love and have faith in it. Trust in each other, above all others. Turn to each other for support, no matter how awful we feel. And we'll remember not to forget why we fell in love in the first place. Even when you try to push me away because you're angry or confused, and you think I don't love you anymore. Even when I forget important details and feel like I have to cover it up. Even when we hit more than a few bumps in the road and convince ourselves that we're no longer happy, because we feel bored or complacent or frustrated with a million tiny things. We'll remember this very moment, and that will be enough to get us through anything."

A tear rolls down her cheek, and then one rolls down mine. She wipes it away with her hand.

"Sounds good to me. I can live with that if you can."

"I sure can."

I remember the box in my pocket.

"Wait, I almost forgot." I reach into my pocket. "I got something for you."

Her eyes widen with interest.

I pull the box out and set it down on the table in front of her. "Happy anniversary."

She turns red and quickly opens it, forgetting in her excitement to try to hide her blush. She stares at the tiny lions as she removes them from the box. She looks at me, her eyes full of love and affection.

"I told you."

"You bought these for me before we met on the train earlier?"

I nod. "Yup."

Her eyes fill with tears once again. "I love them. Thank you."

"You're welcome. I love you, Kate."

"I love you, too." She leans across the table and kisses me, practically tipping our cups over. Everything that's been jarring and crooked and wrong about us, today and yesterday and for the past several years, suddenly feels right again. When our lips finally part, she looks at me and says, "What took you so long?"

I give her a puzzled look, unsure of what she means by that. Then a cell phone rings and startles us both. It sounds like my phone. But where is it coming from?

I glance around, trying to follow the sound.

"I think that's you," she says.

I reach around and feel my pockets, but there's nothing there.

"I thought you said you left your phone at home?"

"I thought I did..." It rings again. I look down at my jacket and see the pocket lighting up with each ring. It's been there the whole time. I look at Kate.

"You gonna answer it?" she asks.

I reach in and pull it out enough to see the screen. It's a local number I don't recognize. "Excuse me a sec," I say.

She nods.

I answer the call. "Hello?"

"Ron?" says a female voice.

"Yeah?"

"Hey... It's me, Courtney."

My jaw drops. My God, Courtney. I forgot all about her. She's still at the house, waiting for me. Expecting to go out to dinner...

"Hey," I respond.

"Hey. Sorry, I know this is probably a bad time, and I shouldn't call you like this, but it'll only take a second."

"All right..." I hold one finger up to Kate. "What's up?"

"I just want to say thanks for taking such good care of me yesterday. It means a lot." Her voice sounds sad and a bit on edge.

"Oh..."

Kate pulls the earrings out and places them in her ears.

"I really enjoyed hanging out with you. You're the best company I've had in a while. It felt really good to be able to talk and feel close to someone like that again. You know?"

I clear my throat.

"I feel silly for even saying this," she says. "But I'm going to miss you."

I try to speak, but I'm paralyzed.

"Hello?"

"It... It's no problem," I say. "Glad I could help."

A moment of silence passes and threatens to suck the life out of me.

"Well, I won't keep you," she says. "I just wanted you to know I made it back safe and sound."

"That's good."

"I'll be moving into my new apartment next week..." Her voice perks up a bit. "So, if you ever need anything... Well, you have my number."

I swallow. "Right."

"Goodbye, Ron. Happy anniversary." She hangs up.

I take the phone off my ear, feeling like a weight has been lifted and moved far behind me. I only hope it's gone for good.

"Everything okay?" Kate asks.

"Fine." I nod, dazed. "Everything's going to be fine." I slip the phone back into my pocket. "Sorry for the interruption. It won't happen again." I look her in the eye. "I promise."

She smiles. "Well, then, what do you say we get out of here and go home? It's been a hell of a day."

CHAPTER SIXTEEN

THE RETURN

I drop some cash on the table and leave the diner with Kate. A cool breeze, trailing in the wake of last night's storm, comes along and chills my skin. Kate holds herself to stay warm.

"Here," I say, holding my jacket out for her. "Put this on."

She thanks me and slips her arms through the sleeves. We look at each other, happy and in love again, like we were the first time we came here.

"This isn't a dream, right?" I ask her.

She looks at me funny. "No, not that I know of. Why, does it feel like a dream?"

I shrug. "Kind of."

"I suppose we wouldn't know even if it was. Would we?"

"No… I suppose not." The thought of it crushes me.

"Until we woke up, that is." She reaches up and touches one of her earrings. "How do my earrings look?" she asks, turning her head side to side.

"Beautiful," I tell her.

There's so much I want to say. Things I want to ask her. But I don't want to ruin it. Everything is perfect right now, and I want to enjoy every moment of it, in case everything falls apart again. I'm not entirely convinced that things are back to normal yet. It all seems too good to be true.

"So...home?" I ask.

"Mm-hmm." She nods.

"Our home?"

Her eyes drift off to the side briefly, as if contemplating what I mean. "Mm-hmm," she repeats.

"Great," I say, breathing a sigh of relief. "Let's do it." I can't believe it. I really have my wife back. I still don't understand anything that has gone on in the last twenty-four hours, but right now, I honestly don't care. I'm getting a second chance.

I reach into my pocket and grab my keys. "I guess I'll meet you at the house then?"

"I guess you will." She steps forward and gives me another soft, meaningful kiss. Her lips taste new and exciting again. "By the way," she says. "Happy anniversary."

I grin and kiss her again. "Happy anniversary, Kate." I frame her face with my hands, gazing into her eyes. "I love you so much."

"I love you too," she says. Then she gives me another quick kiss and says, "Let's go home. I have a surprise for you."

I raise my eyebrows. "You do?"

"Yup."

"What is it?"

"You'll see. Come on."

I wait for her to leave first so she can lead the way. I need to be sure that she knows the way home. If she does, then I'll know all is well. If she doesn't...I don't know. I desperately hope that she does.

I stay close behind her the whole way. So far so good. I'm nervous as hell that she's going to take an unexpected turn and lead me somewhere that isn't our house.

I wonder what the surprise is. Normally I'd be excited, but under the current circumstances it only makes me more nervous. I've had enough surprises for one week.

I can see the back of her head through her rear window, a black patch against the dark gray of the car interior. I watch closely for strange movements. Anything out of the ordinary. It takes me a few blocks to notice it, but it looks like her mouth might be moving. Slight head movement here. Tiny hand gesture there. Like she's speaking to someone in the car, or perhaps using a speakerphone. Hard to tell, but it's making me uneasy. Especially since, as far as I know, she's alone in the car and doesn't have a phone on her.

Anxiety grips my stomach.

I squeeze the steering wheel. She's probably just talking to herself. God knows I do. Or I'm just seeing things, which is even more likely. I loosen my grip, convinced that I'm being paranoid.

We reach a stoplight. The same one I stopped at before my accident yesterday. Her eyes connect with mine in her rearview mirror. I think she's smiling. Good. The light turns green.

We're getting close now. Our street is coming up on the left. She hasn't switched her blinker on yet. Why is that?

My heart pounds. Here comes our street. Still no blinker. She drives past it, and I feel like I'm going to throw up. I knew this was too good to be true. Where the hell is she going?

She takes the next left into a nearby cul-de-sac. The street is dark and eerie. Large trees hover above me, reaching out from behind the houses. She slows almost to a stop in front of a house that I don't recognize. Where is she taking me? Is this where she lives? My hands start to shake.

Instead of stopping completely, she makes a sudden U-turn and then pulls up beside me. She rolls her window down, and I do the same.

"Sorry," she says. "I spaced out for a moment there. I must be more tired than I thought."

I force a smile. "It happens."

"You must have been wondering where the hell I was going."

"I was, actually."

"Sorry." She tilts her head apologetically.

"It's okay."

"Ready?"

"Let's do it," I say.

Her smile fades and she gives me a quizzical look. "Are you sweating?"

I wipe my fingers across my forehead and see that they're covered in a thin sheen of sweat. "Yeah... Had the heat on too high, I guess."

She shakes her head at me and blows me a kiss before she drives away.

Phew. False alarm. I use my arm to wipe the rest of the sweat from my forehead.

This woman's going to be the death of me.

Thankfully, she takes a right onto our street this time. A huge, uncontrollable smile spreads across my face. By the time she pulls into our driveway, I think my face might explode, I'm so happy. I bolt from the car, resisting the urge to do a happy dance.

She steps out and looks at me with curious amusement. "What are you so happy about?"

"Oh, nothing." I kiss her. "It just feels good to be home with you."

I unlock the front door, and we go inside. She takes my coat off and hangs it on the same hook I always place it on. Then she sets her purse down on the chair in the hallway like she always does. Love it.

She sits on the edge of the same chair and slips her shoes off, looking at me. "You okay?"

"Yeah, I'm great."

"You sure? You look nervous."

"I'm sure. Honestly, I've never been better."

She sits up straight and smiles, and the sight of her finally home and happy and mine is almost too much for me to take.

I bend down and give her another kiss. I can't stop. I want to feel every inch of her against my lips. I kiss her cheek. She holds my face tenderly while her big brown eyes hold me in place, keeping me hostage once again. I've never wanted anyone more. I need to feel her in my arms. Feel the warmth of her skin.

"What do you say you head upstairs, get out of these clothes, climb into our bed…and I'll meet you there in just a minute?" She smiles mischievously.

"Is that where I get my surprise?"

She nods. "Mm-hmm."

"Great… Sounds good to me." I grin. "See you soon. Don't take too long." I give her one last peck on the lips and run upstairs, feeling every inch the teenage virgin.

I slip out of my clothes and dance my way into the bathroom, singing and humming. I stand there in front of the mirror, pleased with my own reflection for once. I flex a couple of times and convince myself that I look good. No stressful mirror talks with myself this time. No psych sessions. No self-help therapy. No convincing myself to do the right thing. Everything is perfect.

I splash some water on my face, brush my teeth, swoosh some mouthwash, spray cologne, do another happy dance, and exit the bathroom.

I sit on the edge of the bed and wait.

And wait.

I've been up here for a good fifteen minutes now. What's taking her so long? My nerves tighten as I try to ignore the thought.

It's too quiet.

What if she's gone? What if she disappeared again?

Something thumps downstairs, followed by what sounds like a chair scraping across the floor.

She's still here. There's nothing to worry about.

Someone is here... I assume it's her.

Warm sweat runs down the side of my face.

I open the door and poke my head into the hallway. The house is silent at first, but as I listen more intently, I start to hear voices whispering back and forth.

She's not alone.

I throw on a white t-shirt and some black jogging shorts before heading out to the hallway to check things out. I take my time walking down the stairs, making sure to avoid the squeaky step at the bottom.

I enter the kitchen first. It's dark and quiet. The silence jabs at my gut with quick, sharp punches, and I'm worried that the beating of my heart might drown out the whispered conversation. I want to yell out Kate's name, but I'm afraid of the response I might hear. I hear the dishes in the sink, and it startles me. They're moving ever-so-slightly, sliding against each other in the darkness. I place my hand over my chest and remind myself to breathe.

More voices, only it's not much of a whisper anymore. More like low, hushed tones, rapid and indistinct.

I reach around, struggling to find the light switch, when I hear a door close down the hall. The bathroom, perhaps. I skip the light switch and peek down the hallway instead. The living room light is on.

I make my way toward it. The only sound I hear is my own heartbeat. I feel fainter and fainter as each step brings me closer to the unknown. Who am I going to find in there?

I finally reach the living room. There's a woman standing on the other side of the room with her back facing me, studying the photographs, books, and other miscellanea that are scattered across one of our bookshelves. From here it looks like Courtney. Hard to tell, though. The hair color seems right, but it's up in a ponytail, and she's wearing a purple tank top and black running shorts like she just came from the gym.

I take a couple of steps into the room, dizzy and hardly able to see straight. The floor creaks on the second step. The woman whips around, placing one hand over her chest. Everything is blurry, and my vision is tunneling.

"Ron?" She sounds confused by my presence. "You startled me."

I look around the room, paranoid. Sweat builds upon my forehead.

"Ron, are you all right?" she asks. "You look awful."

I can hear her voice, but I still can't get a clear picture of her. "Courtney? Is that you? What are you doing here?"

The toilet flushes behind me. I turn and look toward the hallway, doing everything I can to hold myself together and not faint. I hear the bathroom door open, followed by approaching footsteps. The woman I presume to be Courtney is now standing next to me. I can see her from the corner of my eye, but I don't look to confirm. I'm too focused on the hallway.

Kate appears in the doorway, rubbing her hands together. Her eyes dart back and forth between us.

I begin to feel weak in the knees and my vision tunnels again as my mind races with questions: Is this my surprise? Did Kate set this whole thing up? Was it all a prank, just like I suspected? It seems absurd. I can't wrap my mind around it. I can't even speak.

"Well, well…" says Kate. "I see you two found each other." I can barely hear her words over the sudden ringing in my ears. "Ron?"

Kate saying my name is the last thing I hear before everything goes black.

CHAPTER SEVENTEEN

THE OTHER WOMAN

"Ron?" I hear Kate's voice, lost somewhere in the darkness. "Ron, honey. Come on, wake up."

I open my eyes. I'm lying on the floor. Kate and another woman are hovering over me, frowning with concern.

"Are you okay?" asks Kate.

I blink a couple times and sit up. "I think so." I'm still lightheaded, but my vision is clearing up.

"Phew!" says Kate, resting her hand against my back. "I was really worried."

I rub the last of the fog from my eyes, feeling considerably better than before.

Kate smiles, and so does the other woman. The other woman who…isn't Courtney at all. I definitely know that smile, though. It's the woman who jogs past me every morning, dressed in her usual workout clothes. Hair in a ponytail. What is she doing in my house?

"What happened?" I ask, surprised by how weak my voice sounds in my ears.

"You fainted," says Kate. "You hit the floor pretty hard. I think you might have another lump on your head."

I look at them both, confused.

"Here, let's get you up," says Kate.

They each take hold of one of my arms and help me to my feet. They continue supporting me, even after I'm standing, trying to keep me steady.

"I think I'm good now, thanks."

They let go. Kate raises her hand and gestures toward the other woman. "Ron, this is Heather. You two haven't met yet, have you?"

I give her another good, hard look. She flashes a friendly smile and I recall how her eyes have a tendency to give away some of the sadness she probably works hard to conceal.

"Not officially, no," I say.

"Didn't think so," says Kate. "Well, Heather lives in the area, and she's basically the coolest chick ever."

Heather laughs and rolls her eyes. "Hardly." She extends her hand to me. "Nice to meet you, Ron. Officially."

I shake her hand.

"She only lives a few houses away," says Kate. "I had no idea. Strange, we've never noticed her before, right, hon?"

"Yeah..." I say. "Strange."

Heather and I exchange glances.

"Or have you?" asks Kate.

Heather smirks.

"No. Not really..." I say. "I mean... I see her jogging sometimes on my way to work."

"Oh," says Kate. Her forehead wrinkles.

"Well," says Heather. "I'm sorry we aren't meeting under better circumstances. I hope you're okay?"

"Yeah, I'm sure I'm fine. I don't know what came over me."
I feel around the back of my head for a new lump. "By the way,
were you here earlier?"

Heather glances around the room. "You mean in the last few
minutes?"

I nod.

"Yeah…" Her tone lingers with uncertainty. "I was. Why?"

"Like, here in this room with me, before I fainted?"

"Yup. You stepped in, I walked over to introduce myself,
and then you just sort of…fainted." She scratches the back of
her head. "Is that how you remember it?"

"More or less…" I look at her. "I sound crazy, don't I?"

Heather smiles. "Just the right amount of crazy." She pats
my arm. "Don't worry, I can relate."

Somehow, this makes me feel a little less ridiculous.

"Well," says Heather, "I apologize for bothering you two so
late in the evening. I'm sure you have better things to do than
talk to me. At least I hope so."

"What *are* you doing here, exactly?" I ask. It comes out
sounding ruder than I intended.

"Oh, well… I stopped by for a couple of reasons, actually."
She looks at Kate.

"She brought my phone back to me," Kate interjects. I
glance down and see Kate's cell phone gripped tightly inside
Heather's hand. She hands it to Kate. "We actually met yesterday in the grocery store," Kate continues. "We started a random
chat about the rising price of milk and whatnot, and that's when
I learned that she only lives a few houses away. Next thing I
know, she's inviting me over for a glass of wine."

I nod. "I see."

"And since you weren't home, and the kids are out of town, I figured why not."

"Right," I say.

Kate and Heather both chuckle awkwardly.

"Sounds a bit odd, I know," says Heather. "Inviting her over when we've only just met. But we just kind of hit it off."

"Right," I repeat.

Kate nods. "Anyway, I left my phone there by accident." She tosses her hands in the air. "That's where it was."

"I would have brought it back sooner," says Heather, "but I only just found it this evening."

"Oh, also," Kate says, "Heather was just telling me about how she's having some renovations done on her house later this month. She can mostly work around it, but she'll need a place to sleep for a night or two."

My eyes flick back and forth between the two of them.

"So I told her she's welcome to stay at our house. She can sleep in our big cozy guest bed. It hasn't been slept in for quite some time and could probably use a little love. You know?"

I give her a blank look.

"You don't mind, do you?" asks Kate.

My mind floods with an image of Courtney and me in the guest bed, our bodies pressed together. Her lips on mine...

"No... That would be fine," I say.

Kate nods. "It just makes sense, you know? We've got that big room that we never use, and it's certainly cheaper than a hotel."

"That's for sure," says Heather.

"Well I guess it's settled then," says Kate. She looks at Heather, and I swear, if I didn't know better, I'd think they were sisters. "Just do me a favor and remind me a day or two before-hand in case I forget. I probably won't, but you never know."

"Trust me," says Heather. "If it's saving me a couple hundred dollars, then I certainly will."

"Good, because I guarantee *this* man will forget," says Kate.

Heather laughs. "No problem. I really appreciate the gener-osity, you guys. It'll only be for a night or two. I promise I won't be any trouble."

"Oh, I'm not worried about it," says Kate, waving her hand in the air. "It'll be nice to have another woman around for once. Someone I can vent to." She looks at me playfully, with an evil eye.

"Tell me about it," says Heather. "God knows we can't rely on men for such things."

Kate laughs harder than necessary. "And please, stop by and visit any time. You don't have to wait until then if you want to hang out. I'm usually here in the afternoons."

"Great," says Heather. "I'll see what I can do. Weeknights are tough for me because I usually get home pretty late, depend-ing on how long it takes me to escape the crazy shit show that is my job."

Kate chuckles.

"Or even better, let's get the hell out of our homes and go downtown for a drink some Saturday."

Kate grins. "I'd love that."

"Or a hike, even. You like hiking?"

"Uh…" Kate stammers. "Not really. But I'm open to try-ing."

Heather nods. "Cool, we'll have to plan something soon. I'll bring my dog, Molly. She loves adventures."

Kate nods and then turns to me like she just remembered I was in the room. She frowns apologetically. "Sorry I left you waiting upstairs for so long. I invited her in after she showed up at the door and we kind of lost track of time."

"My fault, sorry," says Heather, holding one hand up and smiling sheepishly.

I force another smile. Awkward silence slithers around us, growing tenser as the seconds tick by.

"Well," says Heather. "I guess I'll be on my way then. I don't want to take up any more of your time, especially on your anniversary." She grins.

"Yes, indeed," says Kate, grinning back and glowing beautifully.

I smile.

"To be honest, I'm surprised you two still have your clothes on. Back in the day, if you had stopped by my house at this time of night on my wedding anniversary, you never would have made it past the front step because I wouldn't have heard anything past the sound of my own headboard banging against the bedroom wall..." She looks at us both.

I raise my eyebrows.

Kate coughs. "Ex-husband?"

"Yup."

"Sorry it didn't work out. Must have been hard on you."

Heather swipes her hand through the air. "Nah... Screw him. I'm much better off now, anyway."

"What happened?" I say. "If you don't mind me asking."

"Well... Let's just say that after about the fourth or fifth instance of him making it painfully clear that his mind and eyes were on other women, I decided it was finally time to swallow my pride and accept defeat. I let him have what he really wanted, essentially. Whatever that was."

"Right," says Kate. Her eyes drift down toward the floor, then over to me.

"But, hey," says Heather. "I'm learning to be single again, and I gotta tell you, I'm having a blast."

Kate and I both nod.

"Got a date this Sunday, actually. Secret Service guy. Tom. Tall, muscular… Hot." Heather grins.

"Sounds great," says Kate. "What do you have planned?"

"Rock climbing, among other things…"

"Hmm." Kate nods.

"Well, on that note," says Heather, "I hope you two have a lovely evening." She claps her hands together and looks at Kate expectantly. "Dinner plans went well, I take it?"

"Yes, very. It was a very…special night," says Kate, glancing at me with a shy smile.

"That's wonderful," says Heather. "Sometimes you just have to go all out, I guess."

"I guess so," says Kate. "Only happens once a year, after all. Have to make each one count, right?"

"Right," says Heather. "You never know when it might be the last…"

Kate glances at me, then back at Heather.

Heather clears her throat. "Anyway…" She steps past me, brushing her shoulder against mine, and grabs her jacket off one of the hooks, which happens to be the same one mine is on. As she slips her arms through the sleeves, her eyes roam the walls, eventually landing on one particular spot. I follow her gaze to where our family portrait hangs on the wall. It's back, with Kate featured prominently in the photo.

Heather zips her jacket up. "Well, enjoy your night, you two."

"Thanks, girl. See you soon, I hope."

They hug. During their embrace, Heather peers up at me over Kate's shoulder and gives me a small wink before releasing Kate from her grip. Heather opens the front door and hesitates, allowing her eyes to steer toward me one last time.

"Nice meeting you, Ron," she says.

I wave. "Likewise."

"I'm sure I'll see you again soon."

Kate closes the door behind Heather. When she turns around to look at me, her face is beaming with happiness. Like her life is now finally how she wants it to be. Like we've both dipped our feet in new shallow waters, and returned, changed for the better. I still have a million questions, but they can wait.

"All right, Mr. Cordova. I'm all yours." She runs her hand down my chest. "You ready to take me to bed now, or what?"

I smirk. "Yes, ma'am."

"You sure you're still feeling up to it?"

"More than ever," I say.

And with that, I carry Kate upstairs to the bedroom, where we rip each other's clothes off and make love like we're goddamn newlyweds. Every ounce of sweat and saliva we can muster heats up and boils over with desire, running fluently between us and filling the air around us. I hold her face in my hands as if it's gold. Like it's a work of art. A masterpiece. Because it is. We kiss passionately while our bodies become one unified force of nature. Our breath escapes our lungs, then returns, leaping back and forth between our lips. Our love swirls and swoops until finally it bounces off the walls and explodes, raining down all around us, leaving no doubt in our minds that all of this is somehow meant to be. There *is* no other way to be. This is her surprise. *Our* surprise. A reminder that the passion we once felt is still there. It just went missing for a while. It was our job to find it and bring it back, together. And now we're back in full force. This is how we celebrate twelve years of marriage.

CHAPTER EIGHTEEN

THE MORNING AFTER

The roar of water running in Kate's shower engulfs the entire bedroom. I sit up in bed, trying to organize my thoughts as my memories of last night bubble up to the surface of my mind.

Now that we've finally had sex again, and all the pent up frustration has faded, my head is much clearer, and I can think properly.

I glance at the clock. 7:10 a.m. Kate's running late for work, presumably for no reason aside from exhaustion. We were up late. This would probably be an insignificant event in most households, but for us, here, it feels like a major turning point in our marriage. After all, Kate never skips work or runs late just because.

"Do you think you can come home early next Thursday and take Olivia to her doctor's appointment?" Kate shouts over the noise of the shower.

"Yeah, shouldn't be a problem," I yell back.

"I would do it, but there's a parent-teacher conference at Lilly's school around the same time."

"It's no problem," I say again.

"If you want, you can go to that instead, and I'll take Olivia to her appointment."

I picture myself in the school, walking through the crowded hallway, searching for the right room and relying on a poorly designed map to guide me there, trying to get there before the bell starts screaming that I'm late. On the flipside, I picture myself sitting in the waiting room with Olivia, looking through magazines and making jokes about the pictures. Then inside the doctor's office, where we continue to wait, Olivia makes the time go by faster by making me laugh while she sticks her tiny hands inside the large latex gloves and speaks in different accents as she pretends to be the doctor.

"No thanks. I'll stick with the doctor."

"I figured," says Kate.

A few seconds of silence pass while I wait patiently for Kate to speak again. It's only a matter of time.

"So, Heather was nice, huh?" she asks.

"Very nice."

"It was sweet of her to bring my phone back."

"You never told me you went over there and hung out the other day."

Kate turns the shower off and walks into the bedroom with a towel wrapped around her body, drying her hair with another.

She shrugs. "I just forgot, I guess. You got home so late and all…"

But I called her on her cellphone right after I left the parking garage with Courtney. It must have been around six. She was already home by then, making dinner.

"What time did you say you went over there? Right after work?"

She sets the towel down and starts combing her hair. "Yeah, why?"

"And that's when you left your phone there? Before you came home to start dinner?"

"Yes. Jesus, Ron. What is this? An interrogation?"

She generally gets home around noon. It doesn't add up. I shouldn't push the issue, but I feel like I need to.

Our eyes lock together, both of us straight-faced.

"I called you on your cell phone that night. On my way home from work. To tell you I was giving someone a ride home, remember?"

"Yeah, so?"

"So, how did you manage to answer your phone if you had already left it at Heather's house before you came home?"

She sighs and rubs her forehead. "I don't know, Ron. I don't remember every detail of what went on that day. I don't know about you, but I was under a lot of stress. But it happened, and it's over now. So who cares? Do the specific details matter?"

I bring my chin down toward my chest. "No, I guess not."

"Why are you trying to argue with me already?"

"I'm not. I'm sorry. I was so out of it last night... I guess I'm still trying to recall everything that happened."

She nods. "Yeah, I can understand that. How are you feeling, by the way?"

"Fine. Normal."

"That's good. I think." She continues combing her hair. "So weird how you just passed out like that last night. You should make an appointment with your doctor today and let him know what happened, just to be on the safe side. You know?"

"Yeah."

"Get all your new head wounds checked out while you're at it." She smirks.

"All right," I say. "I will."

"It probably wouldn't hurt to get some blood work done while you're there." She sets the comb down and smiles at me.

I smile back. "Thanks, hon."

She nods. "What would you do without me?"

I shrug. "No idea."

Kate removes her towel to get dressed. I stare at her naked body, unsure of how it makes me feel. A bizarre collage of beautiful parts and small imperfections that only I'm aware of, and yet I don't find any of it particularly exciting, or arousing at the moment. Not first thing in the morning, while we're casually chatting, with no anticipation or expectations of making it more thrilling than it is. Perhaps a spouse's body isn't much different than a new car or house, or even a nice piece of furniture that you acquire and keep for many years. It's new and exciting at first, but after a while, it doesn't look like much of anything. It's just simply there. Another familiar item. Funny how that works. That is, until the day comes that it's suddenly gone, and you're forced to realize just how much you've taken it for granted. By that point, it's too late.

She slips her bra on and smiles. "I love you."

"I love you too."

"Last night was wonderful."

"It sure was."

She finishes getting dressed and leaves for work a few minutes later, giving me a kiss on her way out.

I stand by the window and watch as Kate walks down the driveway and gets into her SUV.

Is she really going to work right now? Or is she going somewhere else? To meet with Courtney, perhaps?

Do I know my wife as well as I think I do?

After she drives away, I take a seat on the edge of the bed to collect my thoughts. I need to make some sense of everything that has happened in the last couple of days.

I should have asked Kate where she was all day yesterday. What was she doing when I woke up in bed with Courtney? Part of me is still scared that something will get reversed if I ask too many questions. But how can I not?

I picture Courtney's smile in my head, certain I'll never see her again. It was just one of those things, I guess. Sometimes a person enters your life for no reason other than to get you through a rough spot. To teach you a lesson you didn't know you needed to learn, in order to move on in life. It doesn't make them any less important than anyone else. I think that's how I'll choose to look at this, and let it go at that.

But then why did I think I saw Courtney in the living room last night before I fainted? It felt so real. But it wasn't. The evening we spent together feels similar. Like a strange dream. A timeless moment that exists in a vacuum between the known and the unknown, strong enough to captivate and weak enough to be blown away with a gust of fresh air.

My mind continues skipping along the last couple of days like a movie on fast-forward. I think of Kate in the kitchen, mentioning her appointment with the new doctor. And Courtney on the train, telling me she works in the medical field, but couldn't give me any details. The creepy house Courtney brought me to. Courtney mentioning that Kate works part time when I never told her. Courtney's last words on the phone being

"Happy anniversary." How did she know that? I never told her it was our anniversary.

Then there's the case of the missing phones. The fact that Courtney had my cell phone with her in the car the whole time, because I left it in my jacket pocket. And again, how could Kate have answered her cell phone if she left it at Heather's house? The timing doesn't add up. I don't think that Kate was lying. I certainly didn't see it on her or anywhere near her that night. Ironic though, that both Courtney and Kate were missing their phones on the same day. And that I happened to lose track of mine for most of the night as well.

What about that random phone call Kate received in the kitchen that night, while we were putting the dishes away? She said it was her co-worker, Kay. Whoever that is. Something felt off about it, though. If Kate and Courtney had been working together the whole time, then it's possible it was her that called. And if it was, then she probably used my phone to make the call.

I reach over and grab my phone from the table next to the bed. I scroll through recent outgoing calls. Anxiety begins to creep in. My chest tightens. I look at the list from two days ago, but only see one outgoing call from me at 6:15 p.m. when I called Kate from the car. Nothing after that.

I inhale a much-needed breath. It was worth a shot, but clearly, I'm just working myself up. There are so few connections; I'm looking for patterns that aren't there. I have to let it go.

I take a shower and get dressed for work. Back to my normal, everyday routine. Except now, everything feels different. The routine doesn't feel quite so mundane. I'm much more refreshed.

I go downstairs into the kitchen and brew a cup of coffee to take with me to work. As I lean against the counter, waiting for it to finish, I look over at the phone on the wall. Our home phone. And suddenly, something starts to eat at me.

Call logs are fairly easy to delete or tamper with on cell phones. But on our home phone... not so much.

The coffee maker begins gurgling and choking. I stare at the phone for a second more before grabbing it up off the wall and scrolling through the call log.

My chest tightens again. The coffee maker spits and hisses at me. Liquid is spilling behind me. I had failed to set a mug there to catch it. I stop scrolling when I reach Tuesday night.

Incoming call, 8:13 p.m. on Tuesday night. The only call received that night. That's the one. Only, it didn't come from my phone. It came from a number I don't recognize. I press the call back button.

It rings.

Nobody's picking up.

Soon the ringing stops, and the voicemail picks up: "*Hi, this is Courtney, leave a message after the beep...*"

Panic grips my stomach and squeezes tight. Everything around me stops. I take a step back. Coffee sloshes against my shoes.

It can't be.

Kate.

It was her all along. She did this to me.

Both of them.

I drop the phone on the floor and clench my fists.

What am I going to do? Think. *Think.*

I pace back and forth from the kitchen to the hallway. The family portrait catches my eye in the hallway.

The photo on the fridge. The one of Courtney. It fell on the floor after I dropped it yesterday.

I run into the kitchen and get down on the floor, searching under the fridge. I think I see it. I reach under and pull it out. There it is. I pick it up and look at it, then I crumple it inside my hand.

I need to speak to Kate. I pull my phone out of my pocket and call her cell.

She picks up after the second ring. "Hey, what's up?"

"Why, Kate?"

"Ron?"

"Just tell me why."

"Why what?"

"Why did you lie to me?"

"Lie about what?" she asks. "I don't know what you're talking about."

"You know exactly what I'm talking about; don't bullshit me!"

"All right, calm down and stop yelling at me, or I'm gonna hang up."

"Do you enjoy messing with me? Is it a hobby of yours?"

"Ron—"

"Jesus, I thought you loved me. How could you do that to me?"

"Whoa, slow down. I need you to take it down a notch and chill out. I haven't done anything to you, so what are you talking about?"

"First of all, I have a couple of questions for you."

"Okay…"

"Who called you in the kitchen two nights ago?"

"When?"

"Tuesday night, after I came home late. When we were doing the dishes. You got a call on the home phone. From a co-worker—"

"Okay, okay, I got it. What about it?"

"You told me it was Kay from work."

"Uh-huh."

"But it wasn't *really* Kay, was it, Kate?"

"Yes, it was. Why would I tell you it was, if it wasn't?"

"Stop lying to me, Kate."

"I'm not, I swear. I have nothing to hide."

"So, you're telling me that wasn't Courtney on the phone?"

"Well, no... I didn't say that."

"Excuse me?"

"It *was* Courtney. How do you know her real name?"

"But you just said it was Kay."

"Yeah, because it's the same person. Kay is her nickname."

"I don't understand," I say.

"Her name is actually spelled with a K, but everyone, including her, agrees that it looks awful that way, so she generally chooses to spell it with a C instead. Well, after she told us that we all started calling her Kay as a joke. As in, the letter K."

"All right, enough. I get it."

"What's this all about anyway? Why are you getting so worked up over her name?"

"Kate, I know this may be difficult for you, but for once, I need you to shut up and let me talk."

"Excuse me?"

"Can you do that for me, please?"

After a moment of hesitation, she replies with, "Sure."

I take a deep breath. "So, let me get this straight. Every time you've ever mentioned 'Kay' from work, you were referring to Courtney?"

"Yes, but I still don't see how that is relevant—"

"What does Courtney look like? Give me a description."

"Mm…long, light brownish hair. Sort of caramel colored, I guess. She's a little shorter than me. Petite. Perky. Pretty…"

"Yup, sounds about right."

"You know her?"

"You tricked me, Kate. I didn't think you had it in you, but damn, you really pulled one over on me."

"Ron, listen to me. I need you to listen to me and trust me when I say I have no idea what you are talking about, nor do I understand what Courtney has to do with anything."

"Sure you don't," I say.

"You know what? Whatever. You're obviously very confused. Call me back when you know what the hell you are talking about."

"Kate, she was there the whole time…"

"Who? Courtney? Where?"

My mind starts racing. Courtney calling Kate from my car doesn't prove that Kate betrayed me. But how the hell did she call my house with her own phone. Did she lie to me? Did she have her phone on her the whole time?

"Ron? Hello?"

"Kate, I need you to swear on our daughters' lives that you honestly have no idea what I'm talking about."

"I don't! I swear!"

"Swear to me that you and Courtney didn't work together to deceive me this week."

"Well…"

"Swear to me, Kate!"

"I can't do that…" Her voice softens.

"What do you mean?"

"I admit that she knew what was going on. And that she helped me out."

"Wow. I knew it!"

"I didn't know that's what you were talking about, though. I figured you were referring to something else."

"How could you not have known? What the hell else would I have been talking about?"

"I don't know, Ron, that's the whole point. And what difference does it make if Courtney helped me, anyway?"

"What difference does it make?" I ask. "It makes all the difference. Kate, do you have any idea what you put me through?"

"No, I guess I don't. Why are you getting so upset about this now? You seemed perfectly fine about it last night."

"Last night…was different. Last night, I didn't know the truth."

She snorts. "Could have fooled me."

"It's over, Kate. There's no turning back from this."

"Ron, don't say that. I'm really sorry. I thought you were playing along. Weren't you?" Her voice cracks with desperation.

"Playing along…?"

"And honestly, Courtney hardly had anything to do with it. It was my idea."

"Is that supposed to make me feel better?"

"Tell me what she did to upset you."

I rub my eyelids, ready to have an aneurysm.

"When she called me in the kitchen the other night…it wasn't about anything, really. She just wanted to see how I was doing. She was concerned because of the fight we had that morning. So, yes, I admit, I wasn't honest with you about why she called, but you must be able to understand why I couldn't tell you that at the time." Kate's voice cracks with emotion. With sincerity.

I think of last night at the diner, holding Kate's hand. My own words replay in my mind: *"Trust in each other, above all others... We'll remember this very moment, and that will be enough to get us through anything."*

Trust in each other, above all others.

She's telling the truth.

"Hello?" says Kate, impatiently.

"Damn it, Kate, just give me a second to think."

I slide down and take a seat on the floor, breathing into the phone, and she does the same. It's almost like I can feel her breath through the phone, connecting with mine, bringing us closer together.

Goosebumps rise on my arms. Everything becomes a bit clearer.

Until I get the facts straight, I have to give Kate the benefit of the doubt. I owe her that much. She's my wife. My life partner. My support system. We have to trust each other above all else, no matter how bad things get. Regardless of how sketchy this whole scenario is. No matter how guilty Kate looks. I know in my heart that she wouldn't deliberately deceive me.

Too much of this still doesn't make sense, though. I need to go there and see for myself. I need to talk to both of them, separately, if possible. That's the only way I'll get to the bottom of this.

"All right…" I say. "We're gonna discuss this further, but not over the phone. I need to see you in person."

"Okay."

"Soon."

"Well, I'll be home in like—"

"That's not soon enough. Here's what I need you to do... Do you have any appointments or showings this morning?"

"No, not that I know of."

"Any important meetings you need to attend after eleven?"

"No."

"Good. I need you to leave work thirty minutes early. No later than eleven-thirty. Make up an excuse, I don't care what it is. After you leave, don't go home, go to the Silver Key Diner and wait for me at our usual table. I'll meet you there as soon as I can. I may be a few minutes late, but I promise I'll be there. Can you do that for me?"

"Ron, I really wish you would just—"

"Can you do that for me?"

She huffs. "Yes."

"You have to trust me on this, Kate. I love you enough to trust you. I need you to do the same for me."

"Okay."

"It's important."

"I understand," she says. "I'll be there. I promise."

"Good. I'll see you soon."

"All right..." Her voice softens again, rolling sweetly off her tongue like the Kate I used to know.

"Kate?"

"Yeah?"

"I love you."

"I love you too."

"Oh, and one more thing," I say. "Don't say anything to Courtney about this."

She laughs. "Are you kidding me? That's the first thing I'm doing as soon as we hang up."

"No, don't do that. Don't say anything to her. Not before you meet with me, at least."

"I can't make promises."

"Kate."

"What?" she asks, her voice edged with defensiveness.

"I understand it's in your nature to be stubborn. But if you truly love me, and have nothing to hide, then you won't say anything to her."

She sighs. "All right, Ron. I trust you. I won't say anything. But I hope to God it's for a good reason, because I have a whole lot of questions I'd like to ask her right about now."

"Yeah..." I say. "You and me both."

CHAPTER NINETEEN

SURPRISE VISIT

I park outside of Kate's building at 11:25 a.m., then I sit and wait. I stare up at the building, studying the sixth floor where she works. Where Courtney works too, apparently. My eyes flick back and forth between the building and the clock, my body rigid with tension.

At 11:31 Kate appears in the doorway. I watch her as she walks to her car a couple of rows ahead of me. Even now, I can't help but smile. She gets in her Jeep and drives away. I leave my car and head inside. The hallways appear dimmer than necessary. Not many people around, which is good.

I take the elevator up to the sixth floor. My heart speeds up with anticipation. I see the brown double doors with "Grant and Williams" displayed on the front. I walk through and find Penelope seated at the front desk, wearing a black and white striped dress. Her black hair runs past her tanned shoulders in tight, thin curls.

"Hey, Ron," she says, her tone hesitant, like she's a bit nervous. "You just missed Kate. She left a minute ago."

"I know; it's okay. I just need to leave something on her desk." I stop before I get to the main door. My mind is running.

236 · LUKE P. NARLEE

I step back toward the front desk. "By the way," I say to
Penelope. She looks up at me, her eyes wide with curiosity. "I
couldn't help but notice how you just referred to my wife as
Kate."

She blinks a couple of times. "Oh?"

"Do you remember yesterday? When I called and asked for
Kate?"

She hesitates. "Uh-huh."

"Good. Then perhaps you remember convincing me that nobody named Kate works here and that my wife's name is
Courtney."

She hesitates again. "Uh-huh."

"Great." I nod. "Why did you do that?"

She moves her eyes around the room to evade mine. "I'd
prefer not to say."

"I see." I lean against the counter. "Penelope, it's important
that you tell me why you lied to me. It's extremely important,
actually."

She nods slowly. "Okay…"

"Okay."

I open my eyes wider, waiting for an answer.

She catches her bottom lip with her teeth before answering.
"It was Kay," she says with a sigh. "She put me up to it."

"She did, did she?"

"She told me it was part of a…fun anniversary prank that
she and Kate were pulling on you."

"Fascinating. Was Kate involved in this decision?"

"I kind of assumed. But…now that I think about it, she
never mentioned anything about it."

I nod.

"I'm sorry. Kay said it was all in good fun. That you wouldn't be mad. Are you mad?"

I smile. "Not at you."

She smiles back at me, clearly relieved. "I didn't mean to cause any trouble."

"No worries. It's not your fault. I appreciate your honesty." I glance around the room. "There is one thing you can do for me, though, if you'd like to make it up to me."

"What is it?"

"Courtney works here, correct?"

She stares at me blankly.

"Kay?" I say.

"Oh… Yes."

"Where exactly? Does she have her own office? Or a cubicle somewhere?"

"She has a cube. It's right next to Kate's. On the left."

I walk through the main door and enter the work floor, looking around for Kate's cubicle. Once I see it, I glance directly to the left of it. Unfortunately, I can't see who's in it from here. The walls are too high. I need to get closer.

I walk as fast as I can over to Kate's cube and sit down at her desk. I lean in, bringing my ear close to the cube wall to listen for sounds coming from Courtney's cube, but I don't hear anything. She must not be there at the moment.

Just to be sure, maybe I'll walk past the entrance to her cube and take a quick glance to see if she's there.

I stand up and take a deep breath, hoping nobody will notice me, then I push forward around the back, power walking my way around. I look to my right as I pass the entrance. As I suspected, it's empty. I turn around and stop again when I get to the other side.

I scoot back toward the opening with my back against the wall. Out of nowhere, I hear Courtney's voice. A sense of dread rolls through my stomach. She's talking to someone, and she's getting closer. I turn and go back the other way, hiding on the far side of the cubicle. I hear her moving stuff around on her desk.

I slip back into Kate's cube and listen by the wall again. Courtney's fingers are tapping away at a keyboard. I lean in a bit closer and accidentally knock a book over on Kate's desk. It falls, crashing loudly on the floor. Courtney stops typing.

"Kate?" I hear Courtney say.

I don't move. The typing resumes. I grab a manila folder off of Kate's desk, then I step out and begin to work my way back around. I know I should just leave now, but I have to be certain that it's her.

Slowly working my way back over, I open the folder and pretend to read the papers inside. My heart is pounding so hard I'm afraid the whole office can hear it.

I get back to the opening and stop. She stops typing again. God, please don't walk out right now.

I wait.

Her typing resumes. Here we go. I take a deep breath and lean forward, peering into the cubical.

It's Courtney, all right. The sight of her long, caramel-colored hair is devastating, despite the fact that I knew she'd be there. I want to jump in right now and confront her. Grab her by the shoulders and shake the answers out of her. But it wouldn't be smart to make a scene right here in the office. I'd get kicked out, and nothing would be accomplished.

She swivels around in her chair and makes to stand up, and I throw my body backwards out of view like my life depends on it. She comes zooming out so fast that I don't even have a chance to hide. She goes the other way, mercifully. That could have been awkward.

I'm done here. No need to push my luck any further. I head back to the front desk to talk to Penelope.

"I need a favor."

"Sure, anything."

"I need you to find a way to get Courtney outside and into her car."

"And how do you propose I do that?"

"I don't know, figure something out. Ask her to run an errand or something. Does your supervisor ever send people out to pick things up?"

She shrugs. "Sometimes."

"Well, there you go."

"But it's usually..." She scans the room with her eyes. "Lower-ranking people." She leans in and cups her mouth with one hand, lowering her voice. "You know... Minions."

"Well, today she's a minion. After I leave, let her know the boss needs her to drive somewhere to pick something up. I don't care what it is, or where it is. Just make sure she has to drive her car to do it. Okay?"

She hesitates for a moment more before giving me a nod. "Got it."

I tilt my head. "I'm counting on you, Penelope."

She gives me a reassuring smile. "I won't let you down."

Back outside, I lean against the side of the building and wait for Courtney to come through the door.

A couple of minutes go by, and I start to worry that she's never coming out. Maybe she didn't buy it. Maybe she saw me and knows what I'm up to. Maybe Penelope didn't follow through on her promise.

Then the door opens, and Courtney walks out. She's wearing a peach-colored skirt and a light blue blouse. A white purse hangs on her shoulder. I follow several paces behind her, taking care to keep my steps silent. She unlocks her car, and as she's getting in, I dart around to the other side. I open the door and slide into the car, planting my butt down on the passenger seat. She jumps, eyes wide. "Fuck!" she says, covering her heart. "Jesus. You scared the shit out of me."

I close the door. "Hey, Courtney."

She catches her breath and straightens her skirt out, tugging it down over her legs a bit more.

Looking at her now, I realize she isn't nearly as pretty as I thought she was. In fact, there's nothing attractive about her at all.

"Well, I must say, this is quite a surprise," she says. "I've got to hand it to you, I'm impressed."

"You have some explaining to do," I say.

"I do?"

"Yeah, I'd say so."

She sighs and runs her fingers through her hair, eyeing me as a teasing smile crosses over her face. "It's good to see you, Ron. How are you?"

"Cut the shit and start talking."

She sighs. "There's not much to it, really. I've been working with Kate for about a year now. I like her. She's fun and unpredictable. But I've always thought she was kind of a bitch to you. Based on what I overheard of your phone conversations and the stories she tells me at work." She licks her lips. "You seemed like a great guy to me. Don't get me wrong, Kate speaks very highly of you most of the time. She calls you the best husband ever and tells everyone how lucky she is to have you."

"She says that?" I ask, both surprised and flattered.

"Mm-hmm. That's why I never understand it when she gives you such a hard time. When she speaks to you, it's like she hates you. I've seen pictures of you, so I already knew you were handsome. You seemed like the perfect package. I started to wonder if I could make you happier than she does. Treat you the way you deserve to be treated." She looks at me. "I still think you deserve better."

"You don't even know me," I say.

"I know enough. Especially after the last couple days." She takes a deep breath. "Anyway, Kate came to me Tuesday morning after your big argument in the kitchen. She was so upset. She thought the marriage was over. And then... I don't know what came over me. Everything just kind of clicked. And suddenly I had my plan."

"And what plan was that?" I ask.

"To steal you from her. The idea had crossed my mind in the past, but I never had any intention of actually doing it. But that morning, after she said it was over, I figured...why not?"

"*Why not?*" I repeat, my voice incredulous. The muscles in my body ache from all the tension and stress.

"I knew it had been eons since you two had sex, and like I told you in the car, it's been quite a while for me, as well. And, you being a man, I assumed it wouldn't take much convincing on my part. I figured if she wasn't giving you what you needed, then maybe I would."

I close my eyes and massage my forehead with my fingers. "Jesus..." Is there anything women don't talk to each other about?

"I know it was wrong. And being a friend of Kate's, I knew it was her I should have been sympathizing with when she vented or cried about the problems you two have been having. But it wasn't. It was always you I felt bad for." She looks at me. "I couldn't stop thinking about how much you must have been hurting that morning. I just wanted to cheer you up. See if I caught your eye or not. Or if we had any chemistry. Turns out we did."

"Then what?" I ask impatiently.

"Then… I left work early that day. Took a trip into the city and found you on the train. I knew what train you'd be on because Kate's mentioned it before in conversation. And there you were, fast asleep on the seat. All peaceful and handsome. And that's when I sat down next to you. I could tell you were dreaming. I waited for you to wake up. I was so eager to meet you. I just had to convince you that I had no idea who you were and that it was all a coincidence."

"So, you lied to me. About everything."

"No. Not really. Not about anything important."

"Please…" I say.

"Most of what I said the other night was true. I just told a few white lies here and there in order to…shift the direction of things, so to speak."

I lean back in my seat and rub my head. "Jesus. You're unbelievable." I look at her. "Unbelievable."

She shrugs. "What can I say?"

"So you didn't really forget your purse?"

"No."

"Or your wallet?"

"Nope."

"And you obviously don't work in the medical field?"

"Obviously not."

"And that wasn't really your friend's house we stopped at, was it?"

"No, thank God. Man, how terrifying was that place? It took everything I had to keep a straight face when we first pulled up to it. The look on your face was priceless."

"Did you just pick that place at random?"

"I did, actually. Not bad, huh? I couldn't resist when I saw it. Plus, I figured the chances of someone actually coming to the door were slim to none. You should have seen me when I stood by the front door, pretending to look for my keys. I seriously worried that someone might reach out from the bushes and kill me. I couldn't get back to you fast enough."

"What about coming back to my house with me? Sleeping in my car? Was that all part of your plan too?"

"No, definitely not. Initially, I figured if you took it as far as bringing me home with you, then I'd just wing it and try to make the most of it by surprising Kate. I'm sure your reaction would have been quite something when you realized that Kate and I work together. But I honestly never anticipated you lying to her and telling her I was a man. After that, I decided it was best to go along with your awful plan to leave me in the car for the night. But I was fairly confident you'd come back for me."

I close my eyes, fighting off another headache. "Everything you told me so far is pretty messed up. Borderline stalking, lying to your 'friend,' convincing yourself that you were somehow better for me... It's crazy, but overall, it's still kind of...whatever. Life's tough. Shit happens. I can live with all that."

"I'm glad you feel that way."

244 · LUKE P. NARLEE

"Not so fast," I say. "Let's jump to the next morning. What happened, exactly? When I woke up with you by my side? Because that's the part that's really eating at me, and frankly, still confuses the hell out of me."

"Right...that."

"You obviously knew that you weren't really my wife."

"Yeah..." she says, her tone full of guilt.

"You agree that that's the most twisted part of this whole scenario, right? Like I said, I can live with the rest. I chalk it all up to some wacky, jealous friend shit. But the way things played out yesterday... That's another level entirely. That was just cruel."

"First off, I refuse to take all the responsibility for that. That was mostly Kate's doing."

"So, Kate *was* in on it the whole time?"

"Well, her part of it, yeah, of course. It was her idea. But, she didn't know I was home with you, pretending to be your wife."

"What? I'm still confused."

Courtney huffs, blowing air at her bangs, then combs her fingers through her hair a couple times. "Okay... Early that morning, when I was still asleep in your guest bed, Kate called me on her way to work to discuss her new plan, but she had no idea I was in your house, obviously."

"No, Courtney. Not obvious at all. None of this is remotely obvious."

She rolls her eyes.

"And your story still doesn't make sense. How could Kate have called you if you didn't have your phone?"

"I did have my phone. It was just turned off and...tucked away in a creative manner. Hidden on my person, so to speak."

I stare at her. I have no words.

She shrugs. "What can I say? Women are resilient in tight situations."

"Yeah, I'm learning that."

"I turned it back on after you left me alone in the guest room. But I set the ringer on vibrate and kept it hidden in case you came back. Needless to say, I felt it when Kate called me the next morning. Boy did I feel it." She laughs. Then her joy trails away. "Sorry."

"What would you have said if I had found the phone on you that night?"

"Not sure. I wasn't too worried about it, though. I figured if you got so far as to find it on me, then you'd be too distracted and worked up to care.

I close my eyes, shaking my head in disbelief. "All right, moving on... Kate called you and then what?"

"She told me about the fight you two had the evening before. She sounded panicked. She asked for my advice on what she could do, as a desperate last-ditch effort to save the marriage. She came up with the initial idea, I just helped her develop it."

"What idea, Courtney?"

"She mentioned what you suggested the other morning about starting over. Pretending to be someone else so that maybe you could enjoy each other for once."

"I just meant that morning, during that conversation. I wasn't even serious."

"Yeah, well, she took it to heart. She asked me, 'What do you think about me showing up randomly on his train ride home, only I'll act like I'm a stranger, meeting him for the very first time. Do you think that would turn him on? Reignite a spark between us?'"

I can't help but smile a little. "She asked you that?"

"Ironic, don't you think? Seeing as that's exactly what I did to you the previous day."

"Very. So you encouraged this idea, I'm assuming."

"Sure did. But again, just to be clear," she points her finger. "She thought of this on her own. I just gave her my approval. Though, I admit, I did give her the idea of pretending her car broke down. Figured it would be fun for you if the experience was identical to the one you had with me. Then you could compare the two to see which one of us you enjoyed more."

"It wasn't fun. Nothing about it was fun. It was stressful. And frankly, emotionally abusive."

"To each his own, I guess."

"Courtney, I have a hard time believing that anyone would find that to be fun."

"So you're telling me you didn't get any enjoyment out of falling for your wife again?"

"Yes, of course I did. But that's not the point."

"Okay, but, my point is, if you had to pick a favorite of the two experiences, you'd pick the one with Kate, right?"

"Yes. Of course."

"See, there you go. You learned something important. That's why I encouraged it, while also taking advantage of the opportunity in my own unique way…"

"By pretending to be my wife, and convincing me that I was crazy to think otherwise."

"Well, yeah. Shit, when you put it like that…"

"Courtney…"

"I just wanted to be someone's wife for a day. I knew you wouldn't choose me, anyway."

"You're right; I wouldn't. Because you're a fucking lunatic."

She frowns. "Don't be mean."

"It's not right, Courtney. You told me this last part was all Kate's doing, but without your twisted contribution to it, things would have played out quite a bit differently. I would have dropped you off somewhere the next morning. Then I would have gone to work like normal. Then I would take the train home where I'd run into Kate unexpectedly, only it would have been very obvious to me that she was only pretending to be a stranger, and I have no doubt that it would have been fun to play along. But thanks to you, it was the most stressful day of my life. Even after I found her, it still felt like a heart-wrenching fight to save my marriage and my life as I know it."

"Well, it worked, didn't it?"

"Worked how?" I ask.

"Is your marriage better now?"

"Yeah, but again, that's not the point."

"Sure it is. That's the whole point. I helped save your marriage. One day of stress for a lifetime of happiness. You should be thanking me."

I'm silent for a moment before bursting out into laughter. There's a slight tinge of hysteria to it, but I feel like that's justified. "Thanking you. That's a good one."

"You should!" She crosses her arms over her chest. "I don't see what's so funny about that."

"None of this is funny. And did you really convince Penelope to lie to me?"

"Sure did."

"And what about my mother-in-law? Jesus, I just remembered that. How did you manage to get her involved?"

She shrugs. "I have my ways."

I lean back. "Wow... I honestly don't even know what to say." I look out the window, trying to remember it all. "What about my picture at work?"

"Had it switched," she says.

I look at her, confused.

She blinks a couple times. "I emailed it to someone at your office. I prefer not to say who."

I groan.

"I told you, I'm very persuasive."

I chuckle, delirious. "You're also completely insane."

"Please. Nothing I did was *that* bad."

"Courtney... You stood in my bathroom, naked, and convinced me that my real wife was gone forever. That she was just a dream I had. You watched me fall to the floor in tears, worried about her. And instead of helping me, you lied and pretended to be confused so that you could keep playing wife for a day. That's pretty jacked up, if you ask me."

"All right, I'll give you that. But, for what it's worth, I did decide to do the right thing in the end."

"How's that?"

"I could have easily made things even more confusing and painful for you by pushing it further. I didn't have to stop when I did, after you were convinced things were normal with Kate again. I let you two have your happiness."

"Very kind of you."

I think about sitting with Kate at the diner. It was a special moment. Until the phone rang, that is.

"You called me..."

"I was there inside the diner with you," she says.

"Wait, what?"

"Yup. I was right there, watching you two from another table when I called to say goodbye. Had to witness the magic for myself. See if your marriage was worth saving."

My jaw drops. "You're kidding me."

"I have to admit, you two are pretty cute together. When you're happy, at least. That's why I decided to call and say my goodbyes. I meant everything I said, though. It was really hard for me to do. More than you'll ever know…"

"Incredible."

"That was my way of letting you have your life back. So, again, you're welcome."

"Well, I think I've heard enough. I strongly suggest you stay as far away from me and my family as possible, or I will not hesitate to call the police. I'll get a restraining order on you if I have to."

She scoffs. "You're taking this way too seriously."

"Oh, trust me, I'm taking this *very* seriously. You're lucky you're a woman; otherwise, I would have punched you in the face already."

Her eyes darken with pain. "Stop it. You don't mean that. Haven't you missed me just a little bit?"

"No."

"I wasn't such a bad wife to have for a few hours, was I?"

I shake my head and laugh under my breath.

"I'm serious. Did I do okay?"

I want to say something mean, but the tone of her question is so soft with desperation, I can't help but feel a little bad for her. "Sure, I guess. Under different circumstances, I'd say you were a very good wife. Happy?"

She grins. "Very. You?"

"I will be once I get away from you and resume my normal life again."

"Aww, cheer up, Ronald McDonald. Everything turned out okay in the end. We should be friends. The three of us."

"No. No way."

"Come on, it'll be fun. Might as well, now that the truth is all out in the open. What do we have to lose?"

"We're not friends, Courtney. We're never going to be friends."

"Look how well we get along. We have great chemistry, you and me. Think about it. If you and Kate start fighting again, you'll still have me." She reaches for my hand, but I pull it away.

"Keep your hands off me," I tell her.

"We already follow most of the rules on your marriage satisfaction list. More than you and Kate, I bet. Speaking of Kate... If I were you, I wouldn't tell her about any of this."

"Wouldn't that be convenient for you."

"For both of us. Think about it. I'll start coming over and hanging out with you guys on the weekends. We can have drinks together. Kate will have a much-needed friend outside of work. And if I drink too much, I can always sleep in your guest bed..." She reaches for my hair, but again, I push her hand away.

"You're not getting it. It's over. You're never coming over to my house again, and you'll never meet my kids."

She shifts her body away from me. "Fine."

Kate's still waiting for me at the diner. She's probably worried.

"I have to go." I reach over and open the door, looking at her one last time before I slip out. "Believe it or not, Courtney,

I feel for you. I really do. I think you're a sad, pathetic soul, and I honestly pity you. You need therapy, not a husband. I hope you can find a way to work through your issues that doesn't include destroying other people's lives."

I turn to leave.

"Believe what you want," she says.

I stop.

"But I didn't destroy anything. I'm the reason you're still married, and I'm the reason you two are happy again. Sure, you guys would have kissed and made up regardless after Kate's little role-playing game, but it would have been short lived. Sometimes you have to lose someone completely in order to truly appreciate them. I gave you that. Nobody else did."

I raise my eyebrow.

"And before you walk away all holier than thou, don't forget how much you wanted me the other night. Don't think I couldn't tell, either. All your flirtatious compliments. Telling me how beautiful and sweet I am. What adorable babies I'd make. Staring at my body every chance you got. Maybe I'll have a talk with Kate about that. I'm sure she'd be thrilled to hear all about it." She crosses her arms again, breathing heavy.

"Do what you need to do, Courtney. Just stay away from me and my family." I step out of the car.

"Don't fool yourself, Ron. You're no different than any other man."

"I never claimed I was. Have a nice life, Kay." I slam the door shut.

When I get to the diner, I'm so excited to see Kate that I run from the car to the door, hoping to God she didn't give up on me and leave. I walk in, and there she is sitting at our favorite table waiting for me. She doesn't see me yet. She's wearing a face of concern, chewing on the side of her cheek. As I begin to approach her, she sees me and smiles. Her whole face lights up with relief. I hurry over to her and lean down for a kiss.

"What took you so long?" she asks.

CHAPTER TWENTY

FINAL EVENING ALONE

The following evening, I come home from work and relax on the couch with Kate, flipping through channels and munching on popcorn while she reads a new book on her e-reader. I settle on a basketball game. We're content in the comfort of each other's company, whether we're talking to each other or not.

It's been a long, crazy week, and it's our last night together before the girls come home. I can't wait to see them. It feels like a lifetime since I last saw them. In a way, it has.

Yesterday, after I met with Kate at the diner, we talked for hours. I told her everything. Brutal honesty seemed like the best choice. She admitted that she came up with the crazy plan of meeting me on the train like it was our first encounter. She thought it would spice up our marriage, that maybe a new start was what we needed to get back on track. It was a desperate, gutsy move, but if nothing else, it showed me just how much she loves me, and what she's willing to do to make our marriage work. She dug deeper than I thought she was capable of. Turns out we are Indiana Jones and Lara Croft, after all. She had no idea that I honestly believed she was meeting me again for the very first time, and that I thought it was my one and only chance to win her heart back. She just thought I pulled off a very convincing performance. Whatever works, I guess.

I told her what I knew about Courtney's role in the whole thing, and how I lied about giving her a ride. I told her how I snuck Courtney into the house behind her back while she was sleeping and how she tried to seduce me in the guest bed. I even admitted to staring at Courtney's legs too much. I didn't want to leave out any detail. Kate said she understood, which shocked me, then she half-jokingly agreed that Courtney's legs are very nice. I could tell that she was jealous and hurt by it, but in the end, she forgave me. She said it was a fair tradeoff for all that we'd learned from it, provided that I don't do anything like that ever again. Kate also had a few choice words to say about Courtney—I wouldn't be surprised to see her on the news one night, found in a ditch off the side of the road. Apparently Courtney is now searching for a new job, but in the meantime, Kate is having her desk moved to a different cubicle.

I observe Kate, thoughtfully, while the past few days run through my mind. Eventually she glances up and meets my eyes with a soft, honest smile. She's so beautiful. Her new earrings look amazing on her. I'm going to put full effort into learning how to warm myself by her fire, without getting burned, and she's going to learn how to get her point across without burning me. The hard part is over.

"Did you call about that late fee yet?" she asks.

Some things never change, though.

"No, not yet."

"Are you going to?"

"Of course." I smirk. She smiles back, then returns her eyes to her book.

"Any strange run-ins on the train today?" she asks.

"Nope."

"No strange, flirtatious women popped up, begging for your help?"

"Nope. Not this time."

"Good."

"By the way," I say. "How did your appointment go the other day?" She looks at me, and I can't help but anticipate her frustration and resentment regarding this sensitive topic. "I've been meaning to ask," I continue. "But with all that's been going on..." I wait. Each second of silence feels like an eternity.

She sighs. "It was fine. I met with a new doctor. We discussed the possibility of putting me on some anxiety medication. But in the end... I declined."

"You did?"

"Yeah. I figure it's best to work through our problems head-on, with a clear mind, instead of trying to suppress them and hoping that they go away. You know?"

"Yeah..." Courtney's face flashes in my mind, but the image isn't very clear. I'm already starting to forget what she looks like. "Well, for what it's worth, I think you made the right decision."

"Thanks," she says. "And thanks for asking, as well." She leans in and kisses me softly, her breath emitting subtle hints of passion as she explores my legs a bit with her hands. She leans back and looks at me, flushed. "There's more where that came from."

I smirk. "I can't wait."

She laughs. "See, when *you* show me that you care and make me feel important, *I* show you my appreciation." She glances down toward my lap. "In more ways than one..."

"Hurry up and finish the book. I can look up the score to this game tomorrow."

"Patience, my dear. All in good time."

We go back to staring at our respective screens, the silence infinitely more comfortable than the one we shared just a few nights ago.

"How'd it go with Courtney at work today?" I ask. "You saw her, I'm assuming?"

"Oh, yes."

"What happened?"

"Let's just say…she won't be bothering us again."

I raise an eyebrow.

Kate shakes her head. "I can't believe I ever trusted that little snake."

Her words bring to mind that image of Courtney, curled up in the dark, on the guest bed as the lightning struck.

"You didn't kill her, did you?" I toss a piece of popcorn at Kate's head.

"Maybe." Her eyes peer up at me. She sets her tablet on her lap. "Why? What if I did? Would that make you sad?"

"Yeah. It would."

Her eyes narrow.

"Sad to see you go to prison for the rest of your life!"

She chuckles. "Don't worry, I'm not going to prison." She picks up the piece of popcorn I threw and eats it.

I stare at her, waiting for her to answer my question.

"What?" she says. "I didn't kill her."

"Just making sure," I say.

Her eyes narrow again. "You're awfully protective of her. Are you sure you aren't in love with that girl?"

"Yes, I'm sure. The only girl I'm in love with is you." I press my index finger to her nose, and she smiles.

I'm definitely not in love with Courtney, but oddly enough, I still feel slightly bad for her, now that I've had some time to think about it. I can't imagine how it must feel to be that lonely. Lonely enough to do the things she did. And yet, she did help save my marriage, even if it was in the most bizarre, twisted, roundabout way possible. I think as time goes on, when the wound isn't so fresh and the resentment is all but washed away… I'll be more grateful for that.

I observe Kate carefully again as she goes back to reading her book. I think about how beautiful she is, and how lucky I am to have such an amazing wife. One that would do anything for me. With all the tension between us gone, it feels like a thousand pounds lifted off my back. I've never been happier.

A piece of Kate's bangs falls forward over her face, and I reach up and tuck it back in place for her.

She gives me a warm smile.

I may never know the whole truth of why Kate disappeared from my life for approximately ten hours, leaving me stranded in a life that was so similar and different from my own. In retrospect, the whole situation is so far-fetched, I think part of me may always suspect Kate of being more involved than she claims. It seems like a lot for one person to plan and pull off on her own. Too many coincidences lining up just right. It would have made much more sense if they'd both planned it together from the beginning. The spider and the snake, working together. Maybe Kate asked Courtney to meet me on the train that morning to test me. To see if I would stray if given the opportunity. And Courtney agreed because she wanted to help a friend, but got carried away with her own personal agenda in the process. Perhaps she really had developed genuine feelings for me. Perhaps Kate knew Courtney was in our house. Maybe Courtney took the fall for Kate once she realized I had figured it out. Covered for her to save our marriage. Who knows?

I'll never know for sure. And I'm okay with that. I'd rather choose to trust Kate. All I know is I'm done thinking about other women. I'm done with all the what-ifs. From now on my sole focus will be Kate. And the girls, of course.

"Hey," I say.

"Hmm?"

"We should go somewhere."

"Right now?"

"Soon. Like a vacation. Someplace nice, just you and me. We'll leave the girls with your mom for a couple of days and get away, so we can just focus on each other."

She smiles. "I'd love that."

"Really?"

"Yes, of course."

"Great," I say. "I'll plan it all out. You won't have to do a thing. I'm thinking maybe the beach."

"Mm…that sounds perfect. Whatever you want, though. You know I'll go anywhere with you."

We gaze lovingly at each other.

On the television, one of the basketball players makes a long distance three-pointer. The crowd goes wild.

"I spoke to Heather this morning," Kate says.

Heather… I forgot all about her. "You did, huh?"

"Mm-hmm."

"And what did she have to say?"

Kate looks away at nothing in particular. "I was really close to backing out on our offer to help her. You know, the whole guest bed thing."

"Right."

"That was my plan when I called her, at least. But, in the end, I decided…what the hell."

"What was the deciding factor?" I ask.

"On one hand, it seems a bit risky, considering all that's happened in the past week. But the real reason I was going to cancel is because I remembered that I'll be out of town one of the nights she's supposed to be here. That's the weekend I'm taking the kids with me to my mom's for 'girls' night out.' We'll be back the next morning."

"Ah…" I say.

"You see now?"

"Yeah."

"But I didn't cancel. Because I trust you."

I smile, a bit shocked.

"Also, I thought about what you said about me not having enough friends. And you were right. I shouldn't rely on you for everything. I need more social outlets. I think Heather could be good for me. She's refreshing, you know?"

I nod. "Definitely."

"Now, with that being said, don't think I didn't notice how friendly she was toward you the other night."

I snicker.

"But I'll give her, and you, the benefit of the doubt. For now."

"Fair enough," I say. "But you have nothing to worry about. I've learned my lesson; trust me."

"I hope so," says Kate.

Works for me. As long as this isn't just another test...

I stare at Kate, to read her as she spaces out, lost in her own thoughts. Trying to make sure she's truly on my side. Do I really know her as well as I think I do?

She regains focus and smiles.

It's not a test. I'm being paranoid.

I'm actually looking forward to Heather's visit. Not because she's spending the night or because we'll be alone together, but just to spend more time getting to know her. Purely as friends, of course. There's no reason she can't be my friend as well. Like Kate said, she's refreshing. And fun. It's time to prove that such a thing can happen in the world, without flirtation or any other negative outcomes.

I contemplate sharing these thoughts with Kate, but it's probably best that I don't. After all, there's no need to tell each other *everything*, even when things are going well. She's likely to misinterpret something.

"It won't be too awkward for you, will it? Hanging out with Heather the night I'm gone?"

I picture me and Heather alone at the house. Smiling, laughing. Bottles of beer in our hands...

"Not at all," I say. "I'll be fine."

"Cool." She kisses me.

I will be fine. There's no reason for it to be awkward. And if it does get awkward, then... Well... I guess I'll figure it out when the time comes. Because God knows, life doesn't supply us with a how-to manual on surviving interpersonal dilemmas such as these. So we do what we have to and tread lightly, hoping to find a solution along the way.

ABOUT THE AUTHOR

Luke P. Narlee is a former Air Force member who continues to work for the government as an Intelligence Specialist. He achieved a Bachelor of Science degree in Business Management from the University of Phoenix. He lives in Maryland with his wife, Jane, and their three kids. *Guest Bed* is his debut novel. He's currently hard at work on his second novel, *The Appointment: Lost and Found*; book one of a dystopian, sci-fi trilogy, due to be released 2017.